Folk Tales
of the Highlands

contents

Folk Tales
of the Highlands

by
Gregor Ian Smith &
Alasdair Alpin MacGregor

Lang**Syne**
PUBLISHING
WRITING *to* REMEMBER

Publisher's note

This book was previously published as
Strange Stories and Folk Tales of the Highlands and Islands.

LangSyne
PUBLISHING
WRITING *to* REMEMBER

79 Main Street, Newtongrange,
Midlothian EH22 4NA
Tel: 0131 344 0414 Fax: 0845 075 6085
E-mail: info@lang-syne.co.uk
www.langsyneshop.co.uk

Printed by Blissetts
Design and artwork by Roy Boyd and David Braysher
Cover Design by Dorothy Meikle
© Lang Syne Publishers Ltd 2012

ISBN 978-1-85217-011-0

contents

contents

Cha mhisde sgeul mhath aithris da uair.

A good tale is none the worse for being twice told.

Introduction

The Highlands are rich in folk tales and in the following pages Gregor Ian Smith and Alisdair Alpin McGregor present a selection of their particular favourites. The stories are highly readable and are sure to fascinate readers of all ages.

From the pen of Gregor Ian Smith you can find out about seven brothers who were slaughtered by the Giant of Jura, the princess turned into a goose by witchcraft, the drowned sailors who came back to life as seals, buried mountain treasure, the beautiful young woman who aged seventy years in less than a week, the cloak of invisibility and the vanity of two giants which turned a life of poverty into a life of prosperity for folk living in a glen beside Loch Shiel.

Mr. Smith also tells of the Taynuilt blacksmith who made horse shoes lucky, the piper who vanished near Dunvegan Castle while playing a silver chanter, the water horse of misfortune, a good deed which prevented murder, the Tiree youngster who changed his wicked stepmother into an animal, the clan leader who vowed to build seven churches before his death and the extraordinary strength of Lochaber man Alasdair Cameron.

Alasdair Alpin MacGregor introduces us to a whole host of unusual happenings and events.

The secrets are revealed of creatures like faeries, brownies and water-horses. There are spine-chilling yarns about ghosts and witchcraft. Wells said to cure all kinds of crippling diseases are examined. And to complete the book Mr. MacGregor recalls adventures from the Jacobite Rebellions. This issue consists of extracts taken from the 1937 edition of *The Peat Fire Flame*, published by the Moray Press.

Readers are reminded that certain local comments made in the author's text were of course to conditions as they prevailed at the time of original publication.

PART ONE *by Gregor Ian Smith*

The Little Bannock

Morag, the wife of Donald the crofter at Duntulm, was easily the laziest woman in the island of Skye. She had little to complain of, for Donald's house was small and easily managed, the drinking-well was not a step from the door, and neither child nor dog was there to be dirtying the place. Donald, a patient man, saw to it that peats were always piled at the gable ready for the fire. He it was who tended the two cows, and grew the finest crops in that far corner of Skye. Yet Morag complained and lamented, idling away her time, until Donald was hard put to it to keep from beating her with the porridge-spoon.

One morning she looked round the untidy kitchen. The ashes strewed the hearth, the bed was still to be made, the dishes were unwashed. Even the spinning-wheel was white with dust and cobwebs.

'Dear, oh dear!' she whimpered as she stirred the porridge in the pot. 'It seems that I must work and work and work all my life. And there is nothing I can think of that is more unpleasant!' She thought so much about it that she forgot to keep stirring; the porridge became lumpy and stuck to the bottom of the pot, which made Morag more discontented than ever. And then, quite suddenly, she remembered that sometimes the fairies could be persuaded to come and work for human beings. And was there not a fairy hill at the back of the house, or so it was said!

The lazy woman decided that there would be no harm in asking their help, so she poured the porridge into a bowl, mixed it with cream and set it outside on the step. No fairy, she knew, could resist a bowl of porridge and cream. Indeed there was no better way to tempt the wee folk. So she hid behind the door and waited.

Morag had not long to wait. There was a sudden scurrying and scuffling of feet on the path. The horn spoon began to click against the porridge-bowl. Morag peeped out to see what was happening. Sure enough there they were, a score of them, gathered round the dish, taking turns to sup. Not one of the little people was more than a span high, each was dressed in green and their movements were like the scurrying of mice.

To be sure the porridge disappeared quickly. As soon as it was finished the fairies began to bang on the door until Morag was glad to let them in. 'Good morning', she greeted her visitors, 'I am hoping it is work you seek.'

'Aye and so, wife,' they replied. 'Work we will, but eat we must. So fetch your girdle, mistress, and toast your bannocks. For it is hungry we will be before the day is out.'

Morag fetched the girdle and began to bake oat bannocks, while the fairies went hustling and bustling about the house, as busy as ants. Some swept the floors, some drew down the cobwebs, some hurried to make butter, some busied themselves weaving, while others carded, pulled and teased the wool, until the spinning-wheel was humming merrily. Never in that house had there been so much mending and patching and scrubbing and cleaning!

Meanwhile Morag was busy baking bannocks, until they began to pile up on the kitchen table. But scarcely had they cooled than the fairies stopped their work and ate them up to the very last crumb. This happened so often that Morag was in despair. But she did not dare complain, for fear of being bewitched or carried off to the fairy hill. And so she baked and kneaded and turned her girdle until the last crumb of oatmeal was finished.

Then there was a fine to-do. They clamoured for bannocks until Morag was obliged to go in search of more meal from a neighbour. She ran as fast as she could to the village where she sought the house of the oldest woman.

'What am I to do ?' cried the wretched Morag bitterly. 'My husband has gone to the shieling, my kitchen is full of fairies and they are eating us out of house and home! Tell me what I must do to be rid of them. Grandmother!'

'Tell me first how they found their way across the threshold,' asked the *cailleach*.[1] Morag confessed at last how she had tempted the fairies with a bowl of porridge and cream, so that they would work for her.

'Then let this be a lesson to you, Morag of the white hands, never to trust the wee folk, and never to give way to laziness. Now be off home with you, and when you reach the door open it and cry, "Run, run ! Your house is on fire !" The fairies will run back to the hill. But when they find they have been deceived they will return to your kitchen and carry you off with them.'

'Oh dear,' wailed Morag, wringing her hands. 'Is there nothing I can do to keep them outside? I have no wish to live inside the fairy hill for the rest of my life!'

---

[1] *cailleach*, old woman

'Whenever you enter the house see to it that you upset each thing that the fairies have been using, or else the door that you lock and bolt will be opened for them.'

Morag thanked the old woman, hurried home, and when she reached the cottage she tiptoed to the door and listened. The fairies were all busy. She opened the door a little, popped her head in and cried, 'Run, run! Your house is on fire!' Immediately the fairies stopped their work and came tumbling out of the door, running as fast as their little legs would take them to the fairy hill. Morag skipped inside and locked and barred the door.

Then she went round the house turning everything topsy-turvy. When she had finished she almost wept at the dreadful disorder, for the fairies had left everything in place. But she had little time to survey her handiwork, for the fairies were back again in the twinkling of an eye, screaming outside the door, demanding to be let in again.

'Open the door to us, housewife!' they clamoured through the key-hole.

'I cannot leave the girdle!' replied Morag. 'My bannocks would burn.'

'Open the door, brush that stands by the fire!'

'I cannot for I am standing on my head,' replied the brush.

'Open the door to us, spinning-wheel!'

'I cannot, for my wheel is tied,' replied the spinning-wheel.

Thus did the pots, the pans, the platters, indeed everything that was in the kitchen, reply to the angry fairies, until at length they appealed to a little bannock that had rolled into a dark corner. 'Open the door, little bannock!' they squeaked in their shrill voices, and immediately the little bannock began to roll across the floor.

It skipped across Morag's toes, ran round the table, and would have reached the door had not she leapt over a chair and crushed it to crumbs under her foot. At that very moment she heard her husband's voice outside on the hill. The spell was broken. With a noise like the wind in the chimney the fairies ran off, never to return.

Morag was careful after that never to mention the fairies by name. From that day she gave up her lazy habits and became a good wife to Donald the crofter. But her husband had always great difficulty in persuading her to bake bannocks, which, I am sure you agree, was not surprising!

The fairy cobbler

Ewan Grant worked harder than most crofters on the lands of Alligin on Loch Torridon. Indeed and he had to, for the ground he tilled was sour where it was not stony, the ditches were seldom dry since the rain fell heaviest and the snow lay longest on his side of the mountains. No matter how hard he worked two weeds sprang up where one had been before, and Ewan was hard put to it to make a living.

And so Ewan, the quiet hard-working crofter, remained poor until the day he cast himself on a green hillock to rest his bones and bemoan his lot. Oh, these hillocks and humplocks in the Highland places! Few there must have been that wee folks had not bewitched or put a ring round with their dancing feet. Ewan's couch was green and comfortable, the wind was as soft as the mouse's ear, and the sun warm as the thrush's breast. But there was no rest for him, for there came a tap-tap-tapping to keep his eyes from closing.

At first he thought it was the stone-chat striking his pebbles behind the whins. But no birds were there on the peaceful hillside. Ewan listened closely. The sound came from under his very ear! He peeped into a little hole no bigger than a rabbit's scrape to see a wee small brownie at work at a last mending shoes. As he watched the *Brogaire Beg*[1] yawned. 'Old bones— slow bones! Tired it is I am! Day in, day out and here I sit mending, patching, stitching and nailing shoes for others to wear! Now if I were spry enough to reach the top of Ben Alligin yonder and dip into the treasure crock would I not be the rich and happy brogaire! Aye indeed, but my back is crooked as the fox's leg and my legs shorter than the mole's. Hard enough is it for me to climb into my own bed at night without thinking of reaching to the top of the world!'

Ewan, who was himself feeling much the same as the brownie, listened to every word. He put his mouth to the hole and whispered, 'Good day to you, *Brogaire Beg*, and you might have been speaking for myself. Weary I am with hard work, but my legs will still carry me. If as you say there is treasure at the top of Ben Alligin then maybe I could be finding it for you!'

'Say that again, red-headed man!' cried the brownie, looking up at Ewan, who repeated his words. 'The very thing!' chuckled the wee man. 'Now listen! At the top of the mountain there is a grey stone and a black one, side by side. And in between there is a white chuckie-stone as big as your

[1] *Brogaire Beg*, Little Cobbler

head and seven times as heavy. Put your hand to the chuckie-stone and roll it over. Underneath there lies a crock filled to the rim with gold pieces.'

'If there is,' replied Ewan, 'then I'll put it on my shoulders and bring it here before the sun sets and we will share the treasure between us.'

'You will not!' cried the brownie, tapping Ewan with a stumpy finger. 'You will take from the pot no more than will fill your sporran. And for every piece of gold you take I'll take three!'

Ewan was pleased to agree and leave it at that. So off he went, all weariness forgotten, to the mountain-top, where after much searching he found the grey stone and the black with a great white chuckie in between. He rolled the white stone aside and saw a crock buried in the peat that was filled to the brim with glittering golden coins. It was hard to resist filling not only his sporran but his black bonnet as well with the treasure, but he obeyed the brownie's words and set off down the mountain to Loch Torridon.

The brownie was there to greet him when he returned. And they sat side by side in the sunset counting the gold. For every piece that went to Ewan, three fell in the brownie's lap. But to Ewan's surprise when the gold was divided, by some magic both lots were exactly alike.

'Thanks to me for telling you!' cried the manikin. And hi-ri-ho-ro! - thanks to your long legs, we have gold to take home with us!' And with a skip and a caper the fairy cobbler disappeared into the hillock.

Well, Ewan bought a herd of cows, a score of sheep, hens to lay, a pig to fatten, two chairs, a table, fine linen to cover a new soft bed, and much that I have forgotten. And it was not long before news of sudden wealth was spread abroad. 'Tell me where it came from?' wheedled Finlay his neighbour one day. And foolishly Ewan told him of the *Brogaire Beg* and the crock of gold at the top of Ben Alligin. Now there were greedy men on Loch Torridon, but the greediest was Finlay. Off he went to climb the mountain. On reaching the summit he made haste to find the treasure, rolling each boulder aside until in the end he found the white chuckie that covered the crock.

'Aha!' he cried as he let the gleaming gold pieces spill through his fingers. 'Ewan Grant is the rich man, but there is gold enough here to make me ten - even twenty times as rich!' He filled his sporran, his bonnet, his hose taken from his feet, and his brogues. He made a sack of his tattered shirt and filled it too. Sad he was he could not fill his mouth and his two fists with what little was left. But it could be hidden against his return on the morrow.

With the great weight of gold bending him double he struggled back to Torridon. As he passed the cobbler's hillock he jumped when a squeaky voice cried out, 'You will keep one piece and I'll take three!' Finlay looked down to see the brownie peeping out of his hole in the earth.

'Not a groat shall I give you!' growled the mean man. He was so furious at being seen with his burden that he thrust out his bare foot to crush the life out of the little cobbler. But the brownie was as quick as a weasel, and Finlay's foot struck another hole in the earth. At once the earth fell inwards and Finlay found himself slipping into a giant pit that grew and grew.

With a great fear on him he flung aside first one bundle of gold, then another, until he lay clutching the earth, with only the sporran full of gold left. But the pit opened wider so that to save himself he released his hold on the precious sporran. Immediately he was able to find his way back to the top of the pit where he lay exhausted.

When he opened his eyes again he was astonished to find the hillock exactly as it had been—green and smooth, and with no more than a small scrape that a rabbit might have made at his feet. He ran home as if all the fiends of the darkness were at his heels, and kept the tale of his adventure to himself.

However from that day it was to be noticed that Finlay the crofter became kindly, helpful and generous to his neighbours, and he lived long enough to enjoy a fair measure of prosperity which was perhaps more than he deserved.

The seal-maiden

In the Hebrides and particularly in the islands of Orkney and Shetland, many strange tales are told about the seals. These shy sea-creatures were held in awe by the islanders many years ago. At one time no man could be persuaded to kill a seal, for they were believed to be drowned mariners come back to earth again in the guise of beasts. And certainly for those who have heard the mournful half-human voices of the creatures as they gather to rest on some lonely reef, or plunge and frolic beneath the waves, it is not hard to believe the ancient superstitions.

One tale tells of a young fisherman who lived on Pomona, the old name for the mainland of Orkney. He had gone with several companions to the fishing grounds off the Holm of Boray. It was midsummer, the time of year when the sun's setting makes little difference to the light left in the northern sky. The little fleet made ready and set off in good spirits, for the wind was favourable and gave promise of fine weather.

Before they had gone very far, however, the wind changed. The sky became overcast, and just before sundown a great bank of grey fog rolled in from the sea. The fishermen tried hard to hold to their course and keep together. But one by one they vanished into the gloom of the fog.

The young man drifted alone and in growing fear, for the coasts were treacherous with hidden rocks and endless skerries. Presently the fog grew thinner and he was able to see, a little way off, the outline of a promontory. As he drew nearer he found it bleak and inhospitable. But he was glad to put ashore without further mishap, and he wondered if his companions had shared his good fortune.

After securing his boat against the making tide, he set off to discover where he was and if there was a house near by to give him shelter. He had not gone far before he heard voices and music. It filled him with relief, and he believed he was about to join his companions. Just then he began to notice the skins of seals still wet from the sea laid out on every rock. It was a strange discovery, but the sight that greeted him when he climbed the highest rock was even stranger.

Instead of a group of fishermen gathered about their boats, he saw a great company of strangers feasting and dancing on the shore. Only then did he remember it was the Eve of St John, the night of festival of the sea-folk, when all the selkies[1] swim ashore to cast their skins, and, in the form once more of men and women, spend the twilight hours in merrymaking.

The young fisherman hid himself to watch the revelry, and listen to the music that shrieked and sobbed like the wind on the sea. One by one the stars came out. The mist gathered about the dancers, then vanished on the breeze. And then, when the dance was at its height, the slow sound of the bell of St Magnus' Church came faintly across the sea.

It struck the hour of midnight, the time when the seal-folk must cease their merriment, find their skins and return to the sea for another year.

Beside the fisherman lay a little tawny skin and a garland of brightly coloured seaweed. He could see the figures on the beach transform themselves from humans into seals as they found their skins. Soon the owner of the tawny skin would come. He wondered what form the creature would take.

[1] *selkie*, a seal

He scarcely had time to creep behind the rocks, clutching the skin in his hand, when a maiden crossed the sand. Her hair was tawny as the skin, and her beauty and grace reminded him of the little kittiwakes on the ledges of the limy sea caves. She wound the garland about her hair then began to search for her skin.

When at length she realised that it had gone, and that she could not follow the great company of seals out to sea, she wept. And it was the same sad sound that a seal makes when it comes ashore to suckle its calf. It made the fisherman sad to hear it, but the little seal-maiden had so bewitched him he was afraid that if she found her skin she would leave him for ever.

And so, with the little sealskin safely hidden, he went to the maiden to comfort her. At first she shrank from him in fear, but when she saw he meant no harm, and that she was helpless now without the magic skin, she let him lead her to his boat.

For a day and a night they sailed in the little boat before they reached the harbour of Pomona. The fisherman found his friends already returned from the fishing. They crowded about his boat anxious to know what had befallen him, and he told them of the landfall on the strange island. But he said little of the maiden dressed in the remnants of a sail who accompanied him, except that he had brought her back to wed.

For several years the fisherman and the little seal-maiden lived happily in a humble cottage on the edge of the sea. While he fished or tended his few crops she looked after his home. One day a child was born to them, and the fisherman's happiness was complete. But every year as the Eve of St John approached, the fisherman saw a change come over his seal-wife. Each day when her work was finished and the child asleep she would go down to the sea and listen to the fretting of the waves on the shore. Often she would wait upon the rocks until darkness fell, or until her husband came searching for her. And once when the seals came to play, the fisherman found her weeping bitterly.

When this strange mood was upon her she would wait until her husband had gone, then she would search everywhere for her lost sealskin. But the fisherman had taken care to hide it in the darkest corner of the loft, under a heap of old nets.

One day the fisherman came over the hill to find his little son weeping in the cot, and the fire cold in the hearth. He sought his wife by the shore where she sometimes went to gather the wrack, and across the moor behind the hill. And then he remembered it was midsummer, the Eve of Good Saint John.

He went to the loft, lifted the nets from the corner; the little tawny sealskin was no longer there. Quickly he made his way to the bay where the seals sometimes came to rest. But before he was half-way the sad voices of the seals were in his ears and his heart was heavy.

At the edge of the bay, where the surf broke upon a great ledge of rock, he saw his wife. She was seated with the sealskin on her lap, and the grey seals were gathered about her feet.

He called to her as he ran, pleading for her to remember the infant she had left in the cot, but his voice was blown back over his shoulder. When he saw her rise and cover herself with the tawny skin he knew that she was lost to him. The seals were already edging from the shore, calling to her to follow. At last with a strand of weed about her hair she slipped into the deep water and vanished.

(*The hero of an almost identical tale told in North Uist married a seal-woman who presented him with a large family. This family founded a clan known to this day as* Clann Mhic Codruim nan rón, *'the Clan MacCodrum of the seals'.*)

The Glen of Weeping

Glencoe, sometimes called the Glen of Weeping, is seldom spoken of in the Highlands without recalling memories of the massacre of the MacDonalds.

William of Orange decided to subdue the warring clans north of the Highland line. He ordered that each chieftain appear at Inveraray before the first day of the year 1692, and swear allegiance to the Crown. MacIain, chief of the MacDonalds, misunderstood the order. He made his way to Fort William and on the appointed day presented himself to the Governor, only to discover his mistake. By the time MacIain reached Inveraray four days had passed, four fateful days in which his enemies had seized their chance to take action against the clan.

One month later, on 1st February, 128 'redcoats' drawn from the hated Campbells of Argyll marched into Glencoe. They pretended that there was no room for them in the stronghold of Fort William, and begged food and shelter from MacIain. The old chief made them welcome and entertained them for a fortnight with true Highland hospitality, little knowing the true purpose of their visit.

Rising early in the morning of 13th February Campbell and his men repaid the MacDonalds' kindness by treacherously killing 38 of the clan, and causing almost twice that number to flee into the mountains where they perished in a snowstorm. Yet the fierce blizzard was more compassionate than the king's men, for by detaining a second detachment of troops from Fort William it enabled the scattered remnants of the clan to make their way through the passes to safety.

Many legends have grown round the infamous deed. One story tells of a soldier who learned on the previous day what was in store for the MacDonalds. This man invited his host Maceanruig mer nan Feadan ('big Henderson of the Chanters') to walk with him down the Glen at sunset. When they reached a boulder by the track the soldier stopped. 'Grey stone of the Glen,' he said, 'you have every right to be where you are, but if you could be knowing what will happen here tonight, it is not here you would be staying.' Maceanruig was puzzled, but the soldier would say no more lest he break his oath of secrecy.

When the incident was related to MacIain, the old man would not believe treachery was intended. But Maceanruig and the two sons of the chieftain were suspicious, and they decided to remain awake and alert. The blizzard was at its height when they heard a musket fired. It was the signal for the slaughter to start, and they slipped into hiding. Meanwhile the first cottages were burning and the redcoats on their rounds struck down the unsuspecting families as they slept. One party of soldiers saw a woman running with her child across the moor. The officer in command ordered one of his men to hunt her down and kill her with her child. The soldier soon caught the distracted woman, but instead of putting her to death he led her into hiding, sacrificing instead the dog that trotted at her heels. When he returned with his bayonet smeared with the animal's blood his leader was satisfied that his commands had been carried out satisfactorily.

Many years afterwards an old man came into the Glen. He was given food and shelter by a crofter, and as he took his supper by the peat fire, he heard again the grim story of the killing. When the story was finished he admitted that as a Highlander from Inverness he had taken part in the business. The crofter said no more, but he resolved to take vengeance before the dawn. The old man, however, went on to tell how he had refrained from killing anyone himself. Instead he had secretly helped a woman with her child to escape. But he was unable to tell if they had succeeded in escaping afterwards with their lives.

The MacDonald rose from his seat in amazement. 'Aye indeed they did escape!' he cried, shaking the visitor by the hand. 'That woman was my own mother; and I am the child she bore in her arms. Until the day she died she was praying for your well-being in this world, and for your soul in the hereafter. You are welcome, man of Inverness, to hospitality in this house as long as you please to remain.'

The magic churn

Lachie was nine years of age. He was perhaps small for his age, but there was the strength and suppleness of the willow in his body. And certainly he could run faster than any other boy in the glen, faster even than Duncan his stepbrother, who was fully a year older. This did not please Duncan at all, who was big and rough, and who liked nothing better than to tease Lachie whenever it was possible.

Duncan it was who was sent with the cattle to the shieling, while small Lachie stayed at home to work at the croft. Lachie envied Duncan his days on the hillside in the summer air, for he had nothing more to do than see that the cattle did not stray from the pastures.

One day when Lachie was drawing water from the well he heard someone weeping nearby. He peeped behind the dyke to see a little man buried under a heap of peats that had fallen from the stack. Lachie scrambled over the dyke, pulled aside the peats and helped the little man to his feet.

By this time Lachie was a little bit afraid, for by the green colour of his coat, and the pointed cap and shoes, he saw that this was no mortal but one of the wee folk who lived in the hills. Indeed he would have run off had not the little man caught him by the sleeve.

'Tell me, Lachie,' said he, 'what keeps you here at the croft while Duncan is off at the shieling with the cattle?'

'Today,' replied Lachie, 'I have to draw water to clean the milking pails; then I have to help make the butter.'

'I can make butter too,' said the little man in green, 'the sweetest butter that ever you tasted. Let me see your *muigh*[1] and I will teach you how it is done.'

Lachie showed the little man the butter-churn. It was large and heavy,

[1] *muigh*, a churn

so heavy indeed that Lachie was quite sure the little fellow would not be able to move it one little bit. But the little man made no attempt to lay his hand on it. He sat on a milking stool and began to sing a strange song that Lachie had never heard before. As he sang he rocked to and fro. Meanwhile the basin of cream began to slip from the shelf, tilted slowly and poured the cream smoothly into the churn so that not a drop was spilled.

Next the chum began to rock to the rhythm of the *port a beul*.[1] It began gently at first but soon it was dancing merrily round about, while the cream splashed and slopped inside. In no time the butter was ready. The fairy hopped from the stool, bowed to the bewitched butter-chum and, naming the Five Sisters - which were mountains in Kintail - from east to west, begged it to stop.

Lachie watched with wondering eyes as the little man separated the butter and laid it out in little pats for him to taste. It was as he had promised - the sweetest butter that Lachie had ever tasted!

When Lachie turned to thank the fairy he found that he had vanished. At that moment his parents appeared. When they saw the yellow butter they were astonished. But when they found that it tasted as no other butter had ever tasted they could find no words to praise Lachie for his skill.

From that day Lachie was left to make the butter. The neighbours heard of it, and they too declared that Lachie's butter was the finest in the land. Very soon they came from far and near to buy Lachie's butter until the money in the house over-filled the purses.

But not a word did Lachie say about the *bodachan*[2] and the secret of the churn.

Duncan, as you can imagine, was not pleased with this at all. He grew more jealous of his stepbrother as the days passed. When he demanded to know how Lachie did it the little boy ran off. And as Duncan was slow of foot he could never catch him.

One day he decided to find out the secret for himself. He rose very early in the morning and hid behind a wooden chest. When Lachie came to make the butter he listened very carefully. Lachie sat on the milking stool as the fairy had done and began to sing. Immediately the cream was emptied into the churn, the churn began to dance merrily by itself on the flagstones. By and by, when the butter was ready, Lachie bowed as the fairy had done and, naming the Five Sisters of Kintail from east to west, he begged the churn to stop. When Duncan saw Lachie lay the golden butter pats in rows

[1] *port a beul*, mouth-music   [2] *bodachan*, little old man

upon the shelf he chuckled to himself. 'Now I have the secret. I will make butter too - sweeter perhaps than Lachie's.'

The days passed and soon there was enough cream in the basins to be made into butter. Duncan rose again long before the others were awake. He sat himself on the milking stool and began to sing the song he had heard Lachie sing. Obediently the cream flowed from the basins into the churn. The churn itself began to rock and spin and dance merrily before him. Duncan clapped his hands with delight.

By and by the butter began to appear at the mouth of the dancing churn. Duncan tasted it. It was as sweet as ever. But the rascal was not only sly but greedy. He kept the churn dancing until the butter spilled over. 'I will make butter enough to sell the length and breadth of Kintail,' he told himself, 'then I will be the richest man in Scotland.'

The foolish boy collected the golden pats in basins and in trays. He let it spill on the floor, scraping it together in heaps. The time came when he decided he had made sufficient, then he tried to stop the churn, as Lachie had done, by bowing and naming the Five Sisters. Alas, he had forgotten the order of the names!

Meanwhile the butter came pouring from the churn in a stream that would not be stopped. It rose about him in heaps, waist high, until he could not move.

'Stop! Stop!' he screamed when the wretched stuff touched his chin, afraid now that his greed would cost him his life.

The noise woke Lachie and his parents. They ran to the kitchen Lachie bowed and whispered the magic words, and the churn stopped at once.

The churn was no longer bewitched. No more would it dance merrily as it churned out butter. Lachie was very sad, but from that day it was Duncan who was put to the churning, while Lachie went off on the fine summer days to herd the cattle at the shielings!

Peigi Bheag a Suardail
(Little Polly Flinders)

Peigi bheag a Suadrail
Shuidh i anns an luathadh,
'S ghar i casan beag sa' gliriosach.
Thainig oirre mathair
Is thug i dhi na straicean
Mar shalaich i cuid aodaich cho riasaich.

The witches of Mull

As everyone knows, the survivors of the great Armada from Spain had cause to rue the day they sighted the Scottish coast. Here is a tale from the isle of Mull which concerns witchcraft and how it was used to destroy one of the enemy's ships.

The dwellers on the island were one day stirred to see several fine ships fleeing before a gathering storm. Before the day was out the storm was sweeping the coastline. Angry clouds hid the retreating Armada, and even angrier seas were making it hard for them to find shelter. The night wore on, without any lull in the fury of wind and wave, and it was clear that more than one galleon would never return to Spain.

Dawn came, and with the lifting of the shadows and a slackening tide the wind fell. Watchers searched the strands for signs of shipwreck. All at once a cry went up. A child had found the body of a beautiful maiden cast high upon the rocks of a little cove.

That day the Spanish lady, no less than the daughter of the King of Spain, was buried in a rude grave by the seashore, unattended by priest or mourner, and unmarked even by a wooden cross. Eventually news of her death reached Spain, and the king swore vengeance on a people who had shown so little feeling for a princess as to deny her Christian burial. He turned to an adventurer by the name of Captain Forrest, who professed, among other accomplishments, to have skill in the black arts as well as direct dealings with the Prince of Darkness himself.

When it became known on the island that the ruthless captain planned to pillage every village and dwelling, and destroy by fire and sword every man, woman and child, the islanders gathered to decide what preparations they would make to meet the invader.

The Lord Duart it was who begged that they might match witchcraft with witchcraft. 'Let word be taken to each and every warlock and witch-wife between Mishnish and Erraid, Treshnish and Loch Don!' he declared. 'Let them have word that a wizard seeks to take and hold the island of Mull for himself.'

From near and far came the Doideagan Muileach, the grey witches. Some rode on oat-straws, some flew as daws or carrion crows and many came hidden in the cloak of the wind, until the earth trembled to their fearful clamour. When they were assembled Duart addressed the Doideagan Mor, a haggard beldame whose one eye saw only in the night. He pleaded that a mighty storm be conjured to sink the approaching ship.

'Magic to break magic!' screeched the hag. 'But no magic may destroy that which comes from the hand of God. Has the wizard sought help from the Deity?'

In reply Duart assured the witch that Forrest was an unbeliever. This satisfied the witches and they planned the form the counter-spell would take. Green bracken was brought and twined and fashioned into a rope. At one end a grindstone was fastened, then the loose end was slung over a gibbet-tree. The Doideagan Mor began to pull. The rope tightened, and the stone began to rise from the ground. Almost at once the wind rose, increasing as the stone lifted inch by inch.

But the witch had no more strength to master Forrest's spell. The wind blew no harder and she screamed for her sisters to help. But their efforts were in vain. The weight still hung heavily. Even the muscles of the great smith and his hammer-man were useless.

At last they called for Gormal, the greatest and ugliest of all witches, to come and lay her hand upon the bracken rope. She came on the lightning, a hideous creature with a countenance that hurt men's eyes, and seized the rope. The great stone flew upwards to the summit of Ben More, where it remains to this day, and a storm broke that rocked the earth beneath their feet.

Meantime Captain Forrest's brig could be seen, driven before the mountainous seas, plunging towards the guardian rocks. And as the thunder rolled and lightning seared a sky black as the deepest pit, the ship struck. The Captain and his crew of Spaniards perished, to find a last resting-place on the shores they sought to plunder.

The witches departed in a whirlwind, but the echoes of their victory may still be heard in song and story in odd forgotten corners of the Western Isles.

The giants of Loch Shiel

If you were to walk inland from the shores of Loch Shiel you would come upon a little green glen hidden between the folds of blue mountains. You might be struck by the level fields and the smoothness of the slopes, and wonder why this should be so when in the neighbourhood the glens are rough and strewn everywhere with grey rocks.

Many years ago the little glen was a bleak barren place too, with boulders blocking every path, and heaps of jagged stones and rocks on every hand. The people living in the glen were poor, for there was little soil where crops would grow, and only the poorest pastures to feed their lean cattle.

Half-way down the glen there lived a *seanchaidh* in a small black house hidden against the hillside. Besides being a wonderful story-teller the old man was very wise. One day the young men came to him. 'We are the poorest of our race,' they said, 'because our glen is small and mean, and choked with great splinters of rock fallen from the mountains. Our crops seldom ripen to the full ear, and our cattle are easily stolen by thieves who hide amongst the wilderness of stones. Is there no place where we can live where the hills are smooth and kindly, and the straths are easily tilled?'

In answer the *seanchaidh* rolled aside the stones and loosened the earth. 'There is no finer soil than in our glen,' he replied.

'That may be so,' replied the young men. 'But to clear away the rocks would be a task even for the gods, and we are only men.'

Now, at that time there were giants living in the land. Two great surly creatures lived in the neighbouring mountains, and they were forever quarrelling about their strength. That day the *seachaidh* climbed high into the mists and spoke to each in turn.

'It is a foolish thing to be forever quarrelling,' he said. 'I am but a poor old man, but it seems to me that such a quarrel can be settled easily. Come down into the glen where all the people can see your greatness. And I will set you a task to prove your strength so that it can be seen by all which of you is the mightier giant.'

The next day there was a great rumbling on the mountain-side and the two giants met in the glen. The *seanchaidh* and all the people watched their coming. 'Now let us see who can throw a small stone to the mountain-top,' said the old man.

At that the giants laughed and each lifting a rock as easily as a man would take a pebble from the shore they hurled them into the mountains, far out of sight!

' Indeed, and I have never seen stones fly so far before. But this time let the stones be bigger,' said the *seanchaidh*.

This time the giants lifted rocks seven times the size of a man's head and tossed them easily beyond the mountains. The people heard them rolling faintly into the corries, and they shook with fear.

'It's hard to choose who is the stronger,' said the *seanchaidh*. 'But there are many rocks in this place, and boulders bigger than our own houses. Let us see how many rocks each can throw first with his left hand, then with his right.'

The giants began immediately to hurl rocks far into the air and over the mountains with their left hands. On they went, striding the length of the glen, tearing boulders from the earth, and the noise that rose as the flying boulders sped westwards across the mountains was like the tempests of winter.

Presently they tired of throwing with their left hands. But they continued the contest by throwing with their right hands until the evening came. By then there was scarcely one rock to be seen anywhere. And the giants were so weary they could hardly stand.

'By the Seven Bright Stars,' said the *seanchaidh*, 'there is still no knowing who is the stronger, for we have lost count of what has been thrown. Go you now and look for the rock that has been thrown farthest. And when it has been found bring it to us, and we shall see who can repeat the feat. For only then can we know the mightier giant.'

Still quarrelling fiercely the stupid giants went off in search of the rock that had been thrown the farthest. And for all I know they are searching to this day, for they have never returned. But it is said that the noise of their quarrelling can still be heard when the wind is in the right place.

As for the people in the glen, they made haste to till the soil that the giants had uncovered. And today there are no finer crops growing anywhere than in the little green glen by Loch Shiel.

The witch of Mar

Caitir Fhranagach was a small stooped woman. She was so old that no-one knew her age. And she lived alone in a small dark hovel not far from the castle of Abergeldie.

That she had the powers of evil and witchcraft was beyond dispute. She could bring the storm across the hills in the twinkling of an eye. She could fill the burns in yellow spate when no rain had fallen. Wherever a cow fell sick and died you could be sure Caitir Fhranagach had a hand in it. Few were willing to cross her path or pass within sight of her cottage lest they should come under her spell. The very sight of her crooked form on the road was enough to send the children running back to their homes.

The Caitir had lived so long apart from the rest of the community that she had come to expect neither kindness nor a word of comfort from any quarter, least of all from the Laird of Abergeldie or his fine lady. It came therefore as a surprise when one day the lady crossed her threshold and entered the crone's kitchen.

The Caitir was spinning at the fireside, in the company of a great yellow cat. 'What can the wife of Abergeldie want with Caitir Fhranagach?' she asked without looking up

'I have come for help' replied the lady. 'Let me look into the future, *cailleach*, and the gold I have brought in this purse will be laid in your lap.'

'What is it you would see?' asked the Caitir in a voice that was hoarse as the croaking of the raven.

' I would see my own wedded lord. It is said that he has grown tired of me, and has chosen another. Tell me if the tale be true, and let me look upon the woman he brings from France to live at Abergeldie in my stead.'

The witch heard the chink of gold in the lady's purse, and nodded. She hirpled slowly to stir the fire, then filling a black pot with water, she set it to boil. Into it she sifted ashes, the stalks of plants and a white dust made from the skin of toads. In a little while the pot began to bubble. The steam began to curl up the chimney, and the Caitir drew her creepie close to the flames, rocking slowly to and fro, and murmuring words that were meaningless to the lady waiting by her side.

Presently the steam from the brew began to fill the kitchen like a blue mist. Strange shapes came and went, then a ship appeared out of the vapours. The bright sun shone on its sheets and on the men that moved across its deck. A little apart from the rest stood a tall man and a lady in a crimson gown, at the sight of which the wife of Abergeldie cried out in a sudden fury.

'It is true! Your witch's brew has revealed to me the evil of Gordon. Oh, that you could banish the sun, and raise a storm that would wreck the accursed ship and drown so false a husband!' She flung the purse of gold to the witch, who watched the golden coins spilling across the earth floor. 'Tell me,' she pleaded, 'it can be done, and I will fill the purse again twice over!'

'Lead me to Abergeldie keep, lady,' replied the witch. 'There I can weave a spell to please you.'

The lady made haste with the Caitir Fhranagach, and they reached the castle. The witch slowly climbed a narrow winding stair that ended in a forgotten garret at the top of the highest turret. There she seated herself and ordered that a basin of water be carried to her. A servant brought the basin and set it before the witch. Next she asked the servant to fetch a shallow *cuach*.[1] When this was laid in her hands, she waited until the water became still before floating it in the centre.

She rose and asked that the lady sit where she herself had sat, to watch the *cuach* while she returned by the stairway. At the bottom of the stair lay the dungeon cell, and there the Caitir crawled into the darkest corner. The servant who listened heard the muttering and keening of the crone, trembling as the horrid sounds rose and fell, while in the garret the lady waited and watched as she was bid.

The water in the basin began to tremble. The *cuach* danced gently on the ripples. Slowly the ripples changed into little weaves that leapt upwards, tossing the little craft to and fro. The water hissed and bubbled and splashed over, while the *cuach* rocked and turned over like a ship caught in a storm. When it seemed that the basin must topple over, a great wave leapt up to fill the *cuach* and sent it to the bottom.

The Caitir Fhranagach met the lady in the courtyard. 'It is as you wished, my lady. Abergeldie will never return.'

In the days that followed, the wife of Abergeldie was almost distracted. What the witch had claimed to have done had brought a change of heart. She prayed hourly for her husband and wished for his safe return. But a messenger reached the castle before a week was out with the news that the ship had indeed foundered during a great storm, and all aboard had perished.

Mad with grief the Lady of Abergeldie sent her men to the witch's hovel to put her to death immediately. But the Caitir saw them coming. They

[1] *cuach,* a drinking-cup

closed about the house, broke open the door and entered. But the witch had vanished. All that they saw was her yellow cat in the company of another - a lean black creature that fled through the open door and disappeared into the nearby woods.

A fire was kindled in the thatch, and the cottage was burned to the ground. But the witch had outwitted them, for as the rafters crackled and the flames split the roof-tree, Abergeldie's men heard the Caitir Fhranagach mocking them from the depths of the trees, in the thin wailing voice of a cat.

A' chailleach sa' bhroig
(The old woman who lived in a shoe)

An cual' thu mu'n chaillich
Bha fuireach sa' bhroig?
Bha 'n teaghlach cho lionmhor
Gun rian orr' no doigh.
Thug i dhaibh brochan
Gun aran, gun mharag;
Is sgailc i gu cruaidh iad
'Gan ruagadh do'n leabaidh

Balach beag na deise guirme
(Little boy blue)

' Ille bhig na deise guirme,
Thig is seid an dudach;
An crodh air feadh an arbhair;
Sa' chluan tha na caoraich.
Ach cait a bheil an gille beag
Bu choir bhith toirt an aire orr'?
'Na shineadh ris an dig fheoir
Is srann aige 'na chadal!

The magic milking stool

Nighneag was beautiful: so small, so neat, so very lovely that by the time she reached sixteen she had the lads from all the neighbouring townships worshipping her. She had dark curls that fell to the nape of her pretty neck, eyes that were large, sparkling and of the deepest blue, and lips that were red as rowanberries.

Of course Nighneag knew that she was beautiful, more beautiful than the neighbours' daughters who watched her pass in envy, for did not Alasdair, Murdo, and och, scores of others tell her so when they met! And of course was there not the little mirror by her window to make it plain for her to see!

Nighneag told herself every day that she was much too beautiful and fine a lady to spend her life on the edge of a desolate moor, tending a herd of stupid cows, cleaning a croft-house, toiling with her father in the fields. And sorry am I to tell you, but Nighneag was fast becoming a discontented and stupid young woman.

One day as she went to fetch the cows she was so unhappy she spoke her thoughts aloud. She scolded the cattle, telling them bitterly how much work they caused her, when she might be better employed by the mirror tidying her hair, fashioning new gowns to wear and generally making the most of her charms. I may say that the cattle were well used to Nighneag's sharp tongue and endless complaints. And the fact that they paid not the slightest heed to her made her more exasperated than ever. So that when one day a small voice came out of the heather crying, ' Wait a bit, Nighneag! Let me catch up with you!' she stopped in astonishment. She saw a small woman chasing after her, with a milking stool in her hands.

'Och, och, och, but you go so fast!' gasped the stranger. 'I was hearing your words to the cattle beasts. If it is the milking that is troubling you, see now, I have the very thing - a small wee milking stool,' said the little woman, holding up the stool for her to admire.

Nighneag sighed. It was not a small wee milking stool she was after, but someone to do the milking! Her companion chuckled as she read Nighneag's thoughts. 'Oh, but wait you! It is no ordinary stool at all. Sit you down by the red cow and see what a difference it makes.'

Nighneag shrugged her shoulders, but she laid the stool by the red cow and began to milk. Whereupon she opened her eyes wide, for there was the pail already brimming with milk, and no effort to it at all! Next she milked the white cow and then the black. All in two minutes, mark you, and the cows off to graze again as contented as you please. It was a most extraordinary business altogether,

The stranger was laughing heartily. 'Will you be giving me a small wee promise for my stool, Nighneag?' she asked.

Nighneag would have given her the shoes from her feet for the wonderful stool, but she simply nodded her head. 'Then,' went on her strange companion, 'promise me you will bear gently with the cattle from this day on. Scold them you may, but hurt them neither with hand nor stick, or the three-legged milking stool will have its revenge.'

Well now, that seemed a simple enough promise to keep. Nighneag nodded her head, thanked the stranger and went off with the wonderful stool. From that day onwards Nighneag found milking a pleasure. But of course there were many other irksome tasks throughout the day, and by and by she began to wish she had something or someone to scrub the floors, clean the pots, thin the turnips and feed the hens. And in no time at all she was back where she started, complaining bitterly from dawn to dusk.

One day as she went to fetch the cows she forgot her promise. Old Beth, the red cow, refused to hurry home. Nighneag picked a stick from the hedge and whacked her haunches soundly. All went well until they reached the byre, then Nighneag sat down to milk on the magic milking stool. The stool's three legs began to bend and clatter merrily. Nighneag began to dance up and down as if she were riding a donkey. Over went the milking pail, and Nighneag found herself being carried outside on the runaway stool. And to her horror when she tried to get off she found she was stuck fast!

They danced round and round the croft, through the nettles, into burns and ditches, by thorn and whin and bramble, until Nighneag was blistered, scratched and torn from head to toe. Her shoes were gone, her gown in ribbons and her hair caught into a hundred knots and tangles. At the edge of the moor the stool leapt high into the air, tossing Nighneag into the heather, and disappeared.

When at last she scrambled to her feet, Murdo the herd, Tom the weaver's son and Alasdair from the neighbouring croft had come to see what was happening. What they saw made them stare. From staring they went on to smile. And then they laughed until they very nearly cried.

Nighneag of course was in tears, and she ran as fast as she could to the pool to bathe her hurts. But when she saw her reflection she began to smile too. Then she laughed, and the strange thing was, the more she laughed the better she felt. The stings and scratches became soothed. The tangles in her hair combed out easily, and indeed she began to feel happier than ever before.

From that day, and in spite of having lost the magic stool, Nighneag was happy and well content with her life. A smile was ever on her lips and she sang happily all day. And she became so beautiful that one day the laird's youngest son chose her for his bride, which you will agree is the right kind of ending to so strange and unusual a story.

Simon Simplidh
(Simple Simon)

Simon Simplidh 's Rob nam Bonnach
A 'dol thun na feille;
Thuirt Simon Simplidh, 'Roib, a bhalaich,
Reic iad sin rium fein.'

Thuirt Rob nam Bonnach, 'Ceart a tha thu;
Cait a bheil do sgillin?'
Thuirt Simon Simplidh, 'Siud mo phocaid!
Faic thu, cha' eil gin innt.'

Simon Simplidh chaidh e dh' iasgach
Null gu ceann na bathaich,
'N dull gun glacadh e muc-mhara
'N cuinneag uisg' a mhathar.

The silver chanter

It would seem that not every one of the sons of that famous family, the MacCrimmons of Dunvegan, was gifted with unusual skill in playing the pipes, for one there was, a small slight youth, whose attempts to play disappointed his father. He was the third son, and although his elder brothers could play almost as well as their father, his attempts were no better than those of the tinkers behind the roadside hedge.

He had fine hands, sensitive fingers and a love of good music. But it seemed that it was to be his lot to listen, while his brothers played their wonderful music. Often he would go off to the lonely moors and practise upon an old black chanter, yet it seemed that the improvement would never come. His fingers were not nimble enough, and the music that came was halting and uncertain.

One day he was on the point of throwing the chanter into the depths of a little brown lochan, dappled with blossoming water-lilies, when a maiden suddenly appeared from the shadow of a high rock. There was something in the light that played in her golden hair, in the tilt of her little head, in the grace of her approach, that made the youth a little afraid. Moreover she wore a strange gown of the brightest green, the green of the first rowan leaves, from which came the dye the fairies used (so it was said) to dye their clothes.

'I heard the notes you played on the little black chanter,' she said. 'Let me hear them again, young man.'

Young MacCrimmon apologised for his lack of skill, but the maiden insisted that he should play. When it was over, the maiden smiled.

'What is your greatest wish?' she asked.

'To be the equal of my father as a piper,' replied the youth without hesitation.

'Even if it brings a measure of unhappiness?' asked the maiden.

'Even if it means that, and the life that is in me,' insisted the young man.

'Then take this,' she continued, taking a little silver chanter from the folds of her green gown.

The youth accepted the gift with trembling hands. He had never seen anything so beautiful.

'Now set it to your lips, but let my fingers teach you the notes you must play,' smiled the strange damsel. The youth did as he was bid, while she rested her arms on his shoulders and touched the chanter with her fingers. The music that came was the most beautiful that young MacCrimmon had ever heard.

'Now,' said the maiden when the lesson was over, 'the silver chanter is yours for a year and a day. It will give to your fingers the touch that will make you the greatest piper in Scotland. But you must return with it after a year and a day have passed, to the cave by the little brown tarn yonder where I shall await your coming.'

MacCrimmon promised, and went home with the fairy's gift held tightly in his fingers. But before he reached his father's house the urge came to him to try his skill and play the music the maiden had taught him. To his joy the melody he played was even more wonderful than the one he had learned on the moor. It brought his father and his two brothers to the door, and to be sure, they were astonished at the gift that had come so suddenly to the young man.

'Three sons I have,' cried his father, 'but this one before me is the greatest piper of them all!'

As indeed he was, for his fingers ran on, bringing out sweetness and sorrow and an almost unearthly joy at times from the silver chanter. And when it came to playing the big pipe, there was no doubt of it, there was no man his equal in all the world.

But the day came when young MacCrimmon was duty bound to return the fairy's gift. He set out across the moor with his father and his brothers, until they reached the lochan of the lilies where the fairy dwelt in the cave, But when he reached the shadows of the great rock he halted the others. 'I will go alone now,' he said.

'And when you return, my son, let us hope the magic will still be there in your fingers, even if the silver chanter is no longer with you.'

The young man then went into the depths of the cave, his fingers playing the strangest, saddest music that had ever been heard in the island of Skye, music that had all the sorrows of the world in it, yet was bewitching to the ear. The listeners in the sunshine stood as the piper went deeper and deeper into the earth, his piping becoming fainter. 'MacCrimmon will return no more,' the echoes seemed to say.

And that, in truth, is how the legend must end. For although the last echo never died, but lingers in the farthest passages of MacCrimmon's Cave for those who have the hearing ear, the young MacCrimmon never returned to the earth and the sunshine.

And if you doubt my tale, that MacCrimmon still plays his silver

chanter somewhere in that enchanted cave, then stand in the shadow of the
rock by the lily lochan, which is not so very far from the great Castle of
Dunvegan, and listen. Some say that the sound is the sorrowing of the sea;
others hear in the whisper of music the wind in the young rowan-trees; or
the breath of spring across the waters of the lochan of the lilies. But what-
ever it is, the music is sweet to hear.

Iain Beag nan adhaircean
(Little Jack Horner)

Iain Beag nan adhaircean
'Na shuidhe sa' chuil-mhonadh,
'G itheadh marag mhor na Nollaig,
Stob e steach innt' ordag,
'S thuirt e nuair sin,
'Bu mhi am balach;
Chan 'eil ann cho coir rium!'

Glag ag glaodhaich
(Ding dong bell)

An glag ag glaodhaich cobhair
'S a' phiseach anns an tobar.
Co a chuir ann i?
Co chuir ach Anndra!
Co a thug as i?
Co thug ach Peadar!
Nach b'e sin am peasan crosd'
A dhol a bhathadh piseag bhochd
Nach do rinn de chron air thalamh
Ach sealg nan luch an sabhal athar!

Domhnull and the bay stallion

Domhnull Og was an orphan. When his mother died his father married again. But the second marriage lasted only a few years, and when Domhnull was twelve years old, his father fell ill and died.

The little boy lived with his stepmother in a hovel on the island of Tiree. His life was a hard one. Summer and winter he went barefoot. No work was considered too hard for him, and often he went hungry to bed. As he grew up he came to know the lash of his stepmother's tongue, and the hardness of her heart. He decided to run away as soon as he was old enough.

One evening as he brought the cows home from the pasture he passed close to the shore of Loch an Eilin. A bay stallion was grazing by the waters. The animal was a fine one, unharnessed except for a black bridle, and quite unconscious of the approach of the boy. Domhnull hid behind the foremost cow, and so was able to come very close to the stallion. Then, when the herd came abreast the animal, the lad skipped out and seized it by the bridle.

Now had he stopped to think Domhnull might have been more careful of approaching the horse, for as often as not, such creatures usually proved to be water kelpies. But the boy held fast to the bridle while the creature reared and plunged in its struggles to escape.

When it seemed that the boy must surely be trampled under the flying hooves, or dragged to his death in the waters of the little loch, the bridle loosened. It slipped suddenly from the creature's head, and Domhnull was left holding the bridle while the beast plunged into the loch and vanished.

The lad was disappointed. He would have loved to have captured so fiery and handsome a steed. But at the same time he gave thanks to Providence for being still alive. Besides he had gained possession of a fine, black bridle, such as few boys were lucky enough to have. But, he thought, it would be wise to say nothing of his adventure to his stepmother. As for the bridle it would be better hidden.

He found a cranny in the rocks, and was on the point of concealing his treasure when a voice spoke in his ear: 'Bridle the false one you call *mathair*[1] Domhnull, before the black-cock seeks its roost. From that minute you will be master.' The boy turned in fear and amazement, for it was the bridle that had spoken. Either that or his imagination was playing him tricks. Bridle his stepmother indeed! He would be the bold and foolish one to try

[1] *mathair*, mother

that on the wry-faced termagant! But he determined to take the bridle home with him and hide it in the peat stack.

On reaching the cottage he found the woman dozing over the fire. Softly he made his approach. Surely this was the opportunity to obey the whisper he had heard! He brought the bridle from the folds of his tattered shirt, and dropped it over her head.

She awoke at once, screaming loudly as she struggled to her feet and stumbled outside. But the bridle held firmly in its place. And by the time the boy followed her to the path she had been transformed from human shape to that of a *sheltie*[1] that trembled and pawed the earth. He set his hand on the creature's mane and the sheltie made no attempt to bolt.

The bridle had spoken truly. He had the woman under his spell. Thrice he mounted and rode the animal round the house, and he laughed for joy. He was indeed master and master he would remain, he knew, as long as the bridle held.

But the horse had still to be shod. So Dumhnull set off to the blacksmith, where after many words of admiration had been spoken in favour of the lad's fine horse, he saw to it that the creature was well shod.

From that day the sheltie was put to work on the croft, and each night it came home weary and glad to rest. But it was clear that its spirit was broken. Each day it grew leaner. And in spite of a healthy appetite its hide hung loosely on its bony frame. At length the lad could no longer bear the pain and sorrow in the poor creature's eyes. One morning he took the bridle from its head and threw it far into Loch an Eilin.

In a twinkling the spell was broke. The sheltie vanished, and in its place crouched the cruel stepmother, overcome with weeping. Domhnull bade her rise but she held out her hands and feet. The iron horseshoes were still nailed in place.

The blacksmith was astonished to see Domhnull Og returning to the smiddy with his stepmother shod with iron. He was even more astounded to recognise the shoes he had fitted to Domhnull's sheltie. The boy explained what had happened and the woman begged that the nails be drawn as quickly as possible. At last the blacksmith understood, and set about his gruesome task.

No sound did she make until the last nail was drawn, then the woman uttered a scream of agony, falling in a faint which lasted the night long.

---

[1] *sheltie*, small horse

From that day Domhnull's life was changed. In regaining her human form, his stepmother had lost all bitterness and hatred for her stepson. And the legend ends with the words that they continued to live in that happy and contented state until Domhnull reached manhood and went off to seek his fortune elsewhere.

Highland wit and wisdom

Eallach mor an duine leisg.
The lazy man finds all burdens heavy.

Teagasg ga thoirt do mhnaoi bhuirb, mar bhuille úird air iarunn fuar.
Chastising a termagant is like hammering cold iron.

Is minig a bha 'n donas daicheil.
The Devil is often attractive.

Cha robh math na ole riamh gun mhnathan uime.
There never was good or ill without women being concerned in it.

Nuair is mo a fhuair mi 'sann is lugha bha agam.
The more I got, the less I had.

'Tha biadh is ceol an so!' mar a thuirt am madadh ruadh, 'S e ruith air falbh leis a phiob.
'Here's both meat and music!' as the fox said when it ran away with the bag-pipes.

Faodar an t-or fhein a cheannach tuille is daor.
Gold itself may be too dearly bought.

Socraichidh am posadh an gaol.
Love is soon cooled by marriage.

Seinn port nan sia sgillinn

(Sing a song of sixpence)

Seinn port nan sgillinn,
Mo phocaid lan siol dubh;
Ann am broinn a 'bhonnaich mhoir
Tha corr is fichaed druid.

Nuair chaidh am bonnaich fhosgladh suas
'S ann sheinn na h-eoin le spid;
Nach b'e sin an truinnsear breagh'
G'a chur air beulaobh righ.

Bha 'n righ an taigh an ionmhais
Ag cunntadh suas gach sgillinn;
Bha bhan-righ anns a' chulaist
'S i 'g itheadh mir is mil air.

Bha 'n t-searbhant anns a' gharadh
Cur aodach air an rop;
Nuas druid dhubh le sian
Is spion e dhith an t-sron.

Uis, uis, air an each,
Nighean phapaidh air an each.
C'a ruigidh sinn an nochd,
Ruigidh sinn a bha laidh.
(The foregoing might be sung by a lass riding home on her father's back,
just as a little girl under similar circumstances in England would sing ' Ride-
a-cock-horse.')

Diarmaid and the wild boar

No collection of Highland folk tales would be complete without mention being made of the Feine, a race of warriors whose ancestors were gods. Their hunting ground extended from the land of Erin to the wild mountains of Argyll, and tales of their deeds are almost without number.

The leader of this band was Fin MacCoul. Although he was gentle as the south wind, sweet-tongued and merry, he could terrify the bravest in battle with his strength and valour. This giant among men chose for his bride the beautiful Grainne, daughter of the High King of Ireland. Preparations for the wedding were duly made, and on the morning before the nuptials a great banquet was made ready for the guests.

It happened that Grainne found herself seated opposite a tall handsome young man, and she found her eyes drawn to him. He proved to be Diarmaid, nephew of Fin himself. But she did not know that the *searc*, or love-spot, on his cheek caused all women who saw it to lose their hearts to him exactly as she had done herself.

Before the feast was over Grainne begged the young man to flee with her into the forest. But Diarmaid refused. She was already betrothed to Fin his uncle. Grainne then put him under 'greise', a bond no hero could refuse to honour, and at last persuaded Diarmaid to change his mind.

For many days they journeyed together through dense forests, living frugally on wild berries and animals Diarmaid hunted and killed. Soon word came to him that Fin was in pursuit with his followers. The day came when Diarmaid and Grainne had to hide in a hut, for Fin had at last tracked them down and was determined to kill them both. The hut was protected by a stout fence. Fin set his warriors to guard each side, then called upon Diarmaid to surrender. But Diarmaid had a foster-father with supernatural powers called Angus. On hearing the plight of his foster-child now grown to manhood he made haste to his aid. He urged both Grainne and Diarmaid to make their escape under cover of a cloak of invisibility which he had brought, but Diarmaid refused. Grainne, however, departed under its protection and followed Angus into the heart of the highest forest.

As soon as they had gone Diarmaid called the wind to his aid, and with a mighty leap flew over the heads of the waiting Feine. He reached the forest before Fin could collect his men, and made such speed that his pursuers were left far behind. But the chase was not yet over. Before the day was out Fin and his men were close enough for Diarmaid to hear their voices and the rattle of their swords. This time he chose for hiding a rowan tree in the centre of a glade.

The Feine reached the roots of the tree, weary after the chase, and decided to rest there overnight. But the light still lingered. Fin challenged his son Fergus to play a game of chess. They played until only one move remained on the board, and that move would end the game with Fin master.

Diarmaid, hidden in the branches, had followed the play, and he alone saw the move. He plucked a berry from the rowan and dropped it on the chess-man. Fergus immediately saw the move and won the game.

Fin then challenged his second son Ossian to play. Once again the board was set. Fin played this time with even greater cunning, and as before one move was left to let him win. But Diarmaid plucked another berry. It fell on the chess-man to be moved. Once more Fin was defeated. Fin, however, was suspicious. No-one but Diarmiad of the love-spot could have matched such skill as he had shown and known which piece to move. He looked into the branches and called if Diarmaid was hidden there. No hero of the Feine was permitted to speak falsely, and Diarmaid was obliged to reply.

Diarmaid appeared before the assembled Feine. Fin would have slain him on the spot, but his companions prevailed upon him to forgive his kinsman. Fin agreed reluctantly. Diarmaid then joined Grainne and Angus, and within the span of the moon's journey across the heavens, Grainne and Diarmaid were wed. But Fin never forgave Diarmaid. Before long he persuaded Diarmaid to arm himself and hunt down a wild boar that roamed the hills. The creature had escaped death at the hands of the Feine many times, yet a hero there must be valiant enough to bring about its destruction.

Diarmaid accepted Fin's challenge. The wild boar broke from its hiding-place, but before it could strike with its formidable tusks Diarmaid's spear had reached its heart. Fin pretended to be well pleased. He invited Diarmaid to pace the creature's length as it lay on the grass. 'I am not satisfied, Diarmaid! he cried when the hero had measured twenty foot lengths from head to tail. 'Let it be measured again!'

This time Diarmaid paced out the length of the carcass from tail to head, against the lie of the bristles. In doing so a bristle on the spine pierced his heel. Diarmaid gave a great cry and fell mortally hurt, for the bristle had entered the one vulnerable spot in all his body.

There was yet time to save his life. He called to Fin to bring him a draught of water in his cupped hands. Not even Fin could harden his heart and refuse the wish. He filled his hands at a spring, and was on the point of kneeling before the fallen Diarmaid when he remembered the treachery of the faithless Grainne and the determination of Diarmaid to make her his own wife. The water spilled into the grass, and with a last salute to his old comrades Diarmaid turned away his face and died.

Heigh-diddle-diddle
(Hey-diddle-diddle)

'Mo chreach!' ars a' phiseag,
An cat ag cluich an fhidhill,
'S leum a' bho thar na gealaich le ran;
Lach an cu beag
Ris an spors a bha siud,
'S ruith an truinnsear air falbh leis an spain.

A romance of Loch Leven

Cameron, laird of Callart, lived in a big old house close to the shores of Loch Leven. Mairi his daughter was young and fair. She numbered amongst her friends many of the humble folk in the neighbourhood, and her father, a proud man, disapproved of her associating with them.

One day he saw her talking to a lad from Ballachulish. As punishment she was forbidden to see anyone for a month, her father making sure she would not disobey his order by locking her in her own room. During her imprisonment a trading ship arrived in Loch Leven, bringing fine silks, satin and gewgaws for all to buy. The household of Callart were amongst the first to visit the ship. Mairi in her room waited for their return. They brought with them fineries to delight any maiden's heart, but Mairi was obliged to listen behind the locked door while they discussed and admired their purchases.

Next morning, however, a great stillness had fallen on the house. Neither foot nor voices sounded in the hall nor on the stairs. Mairi could not understand why no-one answered her calls, until at midday villagers arrived in the courtyard. She raised her window to see the lad from Ballachulish in the midst of the crowd. He called to her that the ship had brought the 'black plague' with it, that all in Callart House were either dead or doomed, and that he had orders to burn the house and all within lest the plague spread farther.

Mairi pleaded with him to postpone the burning until word had been taken to Diarmid her lover at Inverawe. Her wish was granted. Diarmid came in the night. He slipped past the guards, who had been posted to prevent contact being made with anyone who still lived within the plague-stricken walls, and threw a stout rope to the waiting girl. Mairi made it fast and descended to safety. Diarmid then told her to cleanse herself thoroughly in the waters of a nearby burn before dressing herself in fresh clothes he had brought for the purpose. By the time dawn was breaking she was with her lover and watching the torches lighted and the great house in flames.

The couple made their way to Loch Awe and Diarmid's ancestral home. But they were forbidden to cross the threshold. Campbell of Inverawe, Diarmid's father, appeared at a high window. He ordered them to stand together, hand in hand, and pronounced them man and wife. Then to make certain they had not been smitten with the scourge nor were able to contaminate anyone by contact, he made them vow they would seek the solitude of a bothy in the heights of Ben Cruachan and remain there alone for forty days.

It was a strange honeymoon following on a stranger marriage. Diarmid and Mairi did as they were bid and lived happily for the rest of their lives together. When Diarmid died of wounds in the battle of Inverlochy years afterwards, a bard of the Camerons put into song the love that Mairi Cameron of Callart had for her fallen lover.

The 'Forty-five'

Of all the famous and historic personalities that have emerged from the history of the Scottish Highlands, that of Charles Edward Stuart, son of James, Pretender to the throne of Scotland, is perhaps the most colourful.

Born in exile on the Continent, the Prince needed only the persuasion of Irish exiles like Sir Thomas Sheridan and Scots advisers like Murray of Broughton to tempt him to sail to Scotland and make a bold bid for the Scottish Crown.

He came in the summer of 1745 on a little ship, the *Doutelle*, after a skirmish in the Channel with an English warship during which the

Elizabeth, a companion vessel, was hard hit and returned to harbour. MacDonald of Boisdale met him on the island of Eriskay where the Prince first landed.

'Go home,' advised the chief who was doubtful of the wisdom of the enterprise.

'I am come home, sir,' replied the young adventurer, and continued his voyage, to land with seven trusted followers at Moidart.

At first it seemed that MacDonald's advice had been wise. The clan chiefs received him with uncertainty, afraid to commit themselves to so uncertain a venture. Even Cameron of Lochiel held back, but in the end he came under the spell of the eager young man who had set his hopes on attaining success. Lochiel and his 700 clansmen accompanied Charles to Glen Finnan, where the Standard was raised.

From then on success seemed assured. The clans rallied, the Jacobite army began to grow in strength, until Lord George, Earl of Murray, the Prince's aide-de-camp, commanded a force of 2,500 men and marched to the capital.

Sir John Cope, who was in command of the regular army, made a half-hearted attempt to intercept the rebels, then turned tail for Inverness. The road to Edinburgh was open, and in a few days Charles had entered the city, opposition having been easily overcome. The heralds raised their trumpets. James VIII was proclaimed king at the Mercat Cross.

Cope returned and approached Edinburgh from the east. With the army at the gates Charles gathered his men and prepared to join battle. After a brilliant charge Cope's men were put to flight by the Highlanders, and he himself escaped to carry the news of his own sorry rout to Berwick.

Had Charles shown wisdom and followed up his first successes by marching straightway into England, history might have read differently today. But he tarried in the city to celebrate his good fortune. From then on disaster followed on the heels of defeat, until the Jacobite army that had marched so proudly across the border, almost to the walls of London, was in the end destroyed and disbanded on Culloden Moor.

Charles retreated to the island of North Uist where he had counted on boarding a ship for France. But the island was well-nigh overrun with soldiers and he himself carried a price of £30,000 on his head.

It is to the credit of the islanders that no-one sought to reveal his presence. Eventually a lady, Flora MacDonald, came to his rescue. She obtained a permit to land in Skye with her maid 'Betty Burke.' The Prince disguised himself in woman's clothes, assumed the name and identity of Flora's maid, and after a perilous journey reached the romantic misty isle.

Alas, it was only to discover that Skye, like North Uist, was a place of danger. He reached the mainland and concealed himself in a cave with seven known robbers as companions. From thence he made his way over the mountains to Ben Aldur. This time his hiding-place was 'Cluny's Cage' a rude hut built of sticks hidden in the trees on the mountain-side, where Cluny himself and Cameron of Lochiel kept his whereabouts unknown for many days.

Not until September 1746, five long months after Culloden, did he manage to make his way to a ship. He sailed from Scotland, never to return, and died an inglorious death in squalor in 1788.

With his departure came a time of sorrow and humiliation for the Highlands. The clan system was destroyed, rights and privileges taken away, and even the tartan which the clans loved so dearly was forbidden as a dress. But the memory of the Young Pretender who had come so near to wearing the Scottish crown, and who had endeared himself to rich and poor alike with his ready laugh and charm of manner, continued to live long after the last bitter defeat of a lost cause.

A highland Samson

The Highlands of Scotland have bred many strong men, and one of them was Alasdair Cameron of Lochaber.

One day Cameron was going home when he overtook a neighbour whose horse and cart had foundered in a ditch. He immediately went to his friend's assistance. The horse was persuaded to try and shift the tilted cart but the animal was too exhausted and went down on its knees. Cameron decided to get the beast out of the shafts. He removed the harness and heaved the horse out of the way. Then he took its place between the shafts, braced his shoulders and dragged the cart from the ditch back to the road again.

'There you are, Murdoch,' he said. 'But I am not surprised the horse could not pull it out. I was hard put to it to do it myself.'

The lucky horseshoe

Iain, the black-bearded smith and farrier of Taynuilt, put his head out
of the smiddy door to see who rode so hard and so fast along the dusty
road. Great was his astonishment to see a giant horse approaching rid-
erless in a cloud of dust. He stood aside in time to let the creature enter
the door, waited until it settled, then made a careful approach to catch
the bridle.

'Make haste, make haste, blacksmith!' cried the horse in a loud
voice. 'I have need of four stout shoes. Already it is past mid-day, and my
journey is still to finish.' The smith saw at once that he had none other than
the Devil himself in his smiddy. Moreover the demon was sore distressed,
with fetlocks streaked with blood, and hooves that had suffered in the ruts
and rubble of the roadways. Iain resolved he would pay dearly for his evil
and misdeeds!

After examining the beast's hooves he addressed the creature. 'I
have shoes to fit. But first I must pare the soles. See that you stand quietly.'
There upon the farrier set the shoes to heat, and began to clean each broken
hoof. Presently he was ready to set the shoes and nail them tight. But by then
the demon horse was squealing and dancing with pain.

'Stop, stop, man!' he cried, trying hard to escape. But the farrier
held him firmly, and proceeded with his work. The beast plunged and reared
in agony. 'Make your terms, blacksmith! Anything that is in my power I will
do, but mercy. I beg of you! Mercy!'

The blacksmith chuckled in his beard, for he knew that he had the
Devil in his power.

'Very well,' he replied. 'But let us strike a bargain. Wherever a
horseshoe hangs upon a door or lintel, let the place within be sanctuary from
all evil, from witch or warlock, or from the Unclean Beast himself. Say ye
so, horse-without-rider, and you shall be shod without further pain.'

The demon horse was so anxious to be gone and free of further pain
at the hands of the righteous blacksmith, that it promised to respect the sign
of the horseshoe. And today the doors are many which bear the charm that
wards off the powers of darkness and the Evil Eye.

Angus Og and the birds

Those who have lived in the north of Scotland will know how long the daylight lingers during the months of summer. Sometimes it seems that the golden afterglow of sunset will last until the coming of the next dawn, and there will be no night at all.

But a time there must be for sleep, and that comes when a great hush falls upon the earth one hour before daybreak.

Many hundreds of years ago, so the legend says, there was no end to the day. Time for sleep was hard to find, for always, day and night, birds would be restless on the moors and in the woodlands, keeping their neighbours awake with their endless singing.

Angus Og, the god of Spring, listened to the voices of the birds, and they displeased him. He could not banish the light, but he decided he must put such a weariness upon the sleepless ones that they would be glad to rest. And this is how it was done.

He summoned all the birds from the moors, the mountains and the glens, and when they were gathered about him on a green knoll he asked which of them was the loudest singer. At that there was a fierce argument, for none could agree.

'Very well,' said the young god, 'from daybreak tomorrow all of you will sing. I will sit on Ben Cruachan, and the voice I hear singing above all others will tell me who is master.'

But there were some like the wren, the owl and the little brown martin whose nests were hidden in holes. 'How will we know when the hour to sing has come?' they asked.

'The red rooster will tell you that,' replied Angus Og, smiling to himself.

Next morning no sooner had the day begun than the red rooster crowed from his perch as Angus Og had promised. First to waken was the lark and he soared upwards, singing his song. He woke the rooks in the trees, the hedge sparrows, thrushes, robins, linnets, until all the birds had joined in the great chorus of song that rang through the forests and far into the mountain glens. Each little bird, even the rook and the jackdaw, made the best of what voice he had.

All through that day Angus Og sat on Ben Cruachan, listening. He clasped his hands, and his laughter was like the wind in the corries, for it was as he had thought. Each bird sang to beat his neighbour, and not one of them could be heard alone.

By sundown the sound of the singing was dying. Even the thrushes and blackbirds were weary and hoarse with their efforts.

'Go to Angus Og on Ben Cruachan,' they told the pigeon, 'and let him tell us who is master.'

But Angus Og shook his head when the pigeon came with his message. 'Indeed it is hard to say. Go back to the birds. Tell them they must sing again tomorrow and every day when the dawn breaks, and I will listen more closely until I have found the master.'

That night, in spite of the long hours of twilight, the birds were glad to rest. But as before the rooster summoned them at daybreak and they tried again. Once more the pigeon went to Angus Og with the message, but Angus Og sent him back with the same reply. Nor did he ever decide who was master, for the singing of the birds made them ready to sleep.

Angus Og still listens to the birds when they sing their dawn chorus. If you doubt the legend, rise in springtime when the rooster crows and you will hear it for yourself. And if you are lucky in the evening, you may even see the wood-pigeon on his way to Ben Cruachan with the question that Angus Og will never answer.

The weasel and the fox

In the woods near Loch Lomond there lived a fox. Besides his share of poultry (which he stole nightly from the good folks' hen-houses) he had a taste for rabbits. This annoyed his neighbour, a little brown weasel, who was of the opinion that the rabbits were his prey and his alone.

Unfortunately the weasel was no match for the sturdy fox, and often the little animal had to go supperless to bed. For the bold fox had on more than one occasion stolen his supper from under his nose. One day as the weasel was hunting the hedgerows he came upon the gamekeeper fast asleep. By his side lay his gun, his snuff-box and five pairs of fat rabbits.

The weasel knew that the fox was not far off. So, one by one, he carried the rabbits to the edge of the wood. He returned for the snuff-box, then went off to find the fox.

'Come and see what a fine supper I have caught,' he boasted.

'And what could a small bit of a weasel be catching that would interest so fine a hunter as me, myself!' scoffed the fox.

'Indeed, and it is ten fat rabbits I have to show you,' replied the weasel proudly. 'Come and see for yourself.'

The fox went off with the little weasel. Sure enough there were the rabbits laid out in a row. 'Indeed you have done well this day,' agreed the fox in evident surprise. 'But tell me, how did you manage it, small one?'

'Och, it was simple enough,' said the weasel. 'I made myself as strong as a man. I sniffed the keeper's magic powder, and in no time at all I had the strength of ten such as you. I found that I could outrun the fastest rabbit. But of course I was not trying very hard to begin with. I contented myself with ten rabbits for a start, and there they are for you to see.'

The fox was very interested, especially in the magic powder that the weasel had mentioned.'Would you care to try it for yourself, my friend?' invited the weasel.

The fox looked at the snuffbox. 'Indeed, and I would,' he replied. If the weasel could catch ten rabbits then he could catch ten times that number.

'Look then,' said the wily weasel, 'open the lid and sniff a very small sniff. And I wager there will not be your equal for strength nor swiftness.'

The fox snatched the snuff-box greedily, opened the lid, and emptied it in one great sniff. Almost at once it seemed his nose had gone on fire! He began to howl in anguish, and his sneezing echoed the length and breadth of the wood.

Meanwhile the weasel had slipped off to where the keeper lay sleeping. He nipped his ear to wake him up, then hid in the long grass. The man rose angrily. He looked around to see what had disturbed him. Then he heard the din from the wood nearby. Clutching his gun he hurried to see what was the matter, leaving the weasel chuckling in the grass.

The little animal listened eagerly. Presently there was a loud bang, and the sneezing and howling ceased in an instant.

That night as the weasel went home he saw the fox's brush hanging by a nail outside the keeper's cottage. It told him that from then on he could catch and eat his supper without a thieving fox stealing it from him. And the gamekeeper was just as pleased, for he had rid the countryside of at least one poultry thief.

An am an eigin dearbhar ne caidrean

(A friend in need is a friend indeed)

Robin Redbreast was caught fast in the thorn thicket. 'Set me free! Set me free!' he pleaded. Two birds heard his cries—the jay and the cross-bill. The jay flew into the wood, afraid that he might be caught himself. But the crossbill set to work to break the cruel thorns, rending and tearing until he had set the captive free.

For his cowardice the jay is despised by birds and man. But the crossbill whose beak became crooked and broken lives happily in the forests of the north. With his crooked bill he is well able to strip the seeds from the cones on which he feeds.

The each uisge

Anna, the little herdmaid, was resting, but she kept an eye on the cattle, especially Peggac the little brown heifer. For whenever the chance came the wayward animal would wander off, taking the herd with her.

So when Peggac suddenly lowed, Anna watched closely. She saw first Peggac then the others rise to stare as a dark shape approached from the lochans. The little girl saw that it was a horse with a long mane and tail, and a coat that was blacker than the *boobrie's*[1] wings. This was puzzling, for she knew of no-one who had such an animal in the neighbourhood.

Next day the horse appeared again, and every day for a week, each day coming closer to the cattle until they paid little heed to its presence. Only Peggac seemed uneasy.

Anna told her parents of the strange horse on the moor. They too were uneasy for they knew that an *each uisge*[2] lived in the lochan where the lilies grew.

'You must run home when it appears, Anna', said her father. 'It is an evil creature out of the lochan. Many a man has been drowned by the *each uisge*.'

[1] *boobrie,* a mythical bird that spreads its wings across the sky at dusk
[2] *each uisge,* 'water-horse,' a demon living in mountain tarns which feeds on flesh

'But it was a great fine creature, father,' persisted the little girl. 'Could we not tame it to fetch our peats from the moor on its broad back?'

'There is but one way to catch and tame such a beast. Seize the halter it wears and it is powerless. And lucky is the man who has such a horse, for it will work without stopping with the strength of ten. Indeed, I would be the proud man if I had the courage to face such a beast!'

Anna saw the *each uisge* every day. By then Peggac the heifer had lost her fear of it. But the *each uisge* was only waiting its chance. One day without warning it sprang towards the little herd, striking down Peggac. Its teeth sank in the heifer's neck and it began to drag her towards the lochan.

The little girl ran for her father, who returned with the dogs and drove it off. But the heifer was dead. He decided that he must find a way to destroy the beast lest Anna herself be taken. He skinned the hide from the dead cow, dried it in the sun, then stitched it up and stuffed it with bracken. Next day he put on the hide himself and lay in the heather as Peggac might have done.

Presently the *each uisge* appeared. It saw the cow that rested on the moor and made its slow approach. The weeds and slime clung to its coat, and a thick halter swung from its neck. When its fiery breath was on him Anna's father grasped the rope and held tight. The creature reared and plunged in a fury to escape. But the man held fast. Leaping up he was soon astride the animal and at once it became quiet.

For many years the black horse lived on the little croft. It was easily managed and worked tirelessly all day. Not once did it attempt to return to the waters of the lochan. And then one day Anna found a halter in a corner of the loft. She decided that such a fine halter would fit the black horse, forgetting that this was the very halter the creature had brought with it from the moor many years ago.

She slipped the rope over its mane and leapt upon its back as she had done a hundred times. For a moment the horse stood still, then with a wild cry it wheeled suddenly and bolted across the moor towards the lily lochan.

The crofter of Duirinish paid dearly for his folly, for Anna was never seen again.

Ailean nan Creach and the cats

Ailean nan Creach[1], chief of Clan Cameron, was a great warrior, and in his day he had brought about the death of many men. One day he had a premonition of his own end, and the prospect gave him cause to repent of his earlier misdeeds.

He went secretly to the house of a witch and begged her help to save his soul from purgatory. The witch heard his confession, then told him what he must do on the morrow.

Ailean took her advice. With one of his clansmen, a sack of peats and sticks, and a cat from his own kitchen, he journeyed far across the moors until he reached a small green field. There he kindled a great fire, and when the fire was at its reddest he hung the cat over the blaze to roast it. There was no man there to witness the deed save the clansman, and he kept a sharp look-out for intruders.

But the unhappy cat let the world know of its plight, and in answer to its cries, all the cats in the Cameron country made haste to the spot. Ailean and his man were hard pressed to save their lives, but they succeeded in keeping the horde at bay, until a large black monster of a cat arrived and demanded an explanation.

Ailean nan Creach told the cat that by singeing the creature that hung over the fire he was atoning for his evil past. The giant cat spat contemptuously. 'Release my brother at once. There is another and a better way to make penance, Ailean nan Creach. For each of the forays you led as conqueror, see to it that a church is built to the glory of God.'

Ailean doubted the great cat, but he saw that if he continued to roast the other, he and his man would be slain on the spot. 'I swear to build seven churches before I die,' he said at length, and released the howling creature by the fire.

Off went all the cats in a wild gallop, led by their still smouldering companion, and they never stopped until they reached the river Lochy. One after another they leapt into a pool. When they saw that Ailean's victim had quite recovered, they swam to the shore and made their way home.

Cameron kept his word. And when he died seven churches stood where no church had stood before, at Kill-a-choreill, Kildonan, Loch Leven, Kilmallie, Kilchoan, Kilkellen and Morven.

---

[1] *Ailean nan Creach*, Alan of the Forays

The grey goose

The owl on silent wings, with its mysterious voice crying in the dusk, was ever a bird of ill omen. Like the raven, the grey crow and others of their kind, it was supposed to presage disaster and doom. On the other hand the robin and its companion Jenny Wren were welcomed by everyone and held dear in song and story. But the swan and the Wild goose, night-flying against the moon, trumpeting their stirring music out of the dark heavens, roused the imagination in a different way, and gave rise to many legends of romance and high adventure.

One day, so the *cailleachs* tell, a king fell foul of a grisly beldame, a witch within whose bubbling cauldron lay the vilest spells. This foul creature took her revenge by waylaying the king's daughter as she walked by the shores of Loch Sunart. She ringed the maiden within a magic circle, transforming her into a grey goose[1] that spread its wings and flew northwards to the land of ice and snow.

No-one knew what had befallen the maiden save the witch. She was sought far and wide for many months, but in the end the search was abandoned. It was believed that she had been devoured by the wolves, or spirited away by the fairy folk. But the princess had a lover, a fair prince, and he continued to seek her in the mountains and the forests. For a year he roamed far and wide, living on the birds of the air, the animals of the woodlands and the fish in the river. He was a mighty hunter whose skill with the bow was uncanny, and it was not hard for him to strike down the hindmost goose in the gaggle that flew one evening across the saltings.

It fell mortally wounded not far from him, and he strode quickly to gather his prize. He readied the bird as the breath left its body. At that instant its form changed, and the young man was horrified to find himself bending over the still form of his beloved princess. In despair he plucked the arrow from her heart, breaking it in three pieces, grinding them underfoot. Tenderly he laid his plaid over her and knelt to mourn his beloved.

Meantime the geese flew in wide circles calling their stricken companion to join them. But the prince heard nothing for he had died as he knelt in sorrow over his princess. The life that had passed from him entered the body of the princess. She stirred as if rising from a deep sleep, once again assuming the form of a goose that spread its pinions in answer to the summons of its kind.

[1] *grey goose*, greylag goose

From the broken arrow grew the first trees of the mighty forest of Caledon. The plaid that had lain over the princess became a broad green sward still to be seen on upper Speyside. And when the stars crackle with winter frost, the voice of a lonely grey goose can still be heard calling down the valleys of the high Grampians.

Meileag! A chaora dhubh
(Baa, baa, black sheep)

Meileag! A chaora dhubh,
Bheil cloimh agad an drasd'?
Tha, dhuin'-uasail, sin agam.
Tri poca lan -
Aon do'n mhaishistir,
Aon do bhean-an-taighe,
Is aon do'n a ghille bheag
Tha fuireach san t-sraid chuil.

A legend of Macfie

This tale is heard in so many forms that it would be rash to say that what follows is nearest of them all to the truth.

Macfie of Colonsay was a strong man and a mighty hunter. He had seven sons, all of them tall and comely. As befitted islesmen they were skilled in the sailing of boats, and often the chief's galley could be seen on its way to Jura or some neighbouring island where the hunting was good.

One day Macfie himself was returning from the moors of Colonsay. Darkness had fallen early, and mist had come in from the sea, so that Macfie was hard put to it to find his way. When it seemed that he would have to seek some corner to shelter until the dawn came, he stumbled upon a small grey house set against the hillside. Macfie knew every inch of the island but he had no recollection of having seen this *bochan*[1] before. But darkness and mist change the form and colour of familiar things and he laid the fault on

[1] *bochan*, small cottage

his bad memory. He peered in the window to see an old woman stirring porridge by the fire.

He was a hungry man, and he presented himself to the crone and begged a bite of food and a bed for the night. He was made welcome (indeed it seemed that his visit had been awaited), and a bowl of porridge was set for him. While he supped, his eye fell on a great hound that lay with two pups in a dark corner.

'My mind is failing me, for surely I have never seen that hound before,' he remarked.

'That may be,' replied the old woman, 'for the hound is lame and cannot travel far. But once she hunted with the strength of the lion and the eye of the eagle.' The old woman then went on to relate ancient tales of how the great hound had outstripped all others in courage and cunning at the chase. Macfie's interest was kindled at once.

'So valiant a mother must surely have borne whelps to match her in speed and courage,' he said, looking closely at the sleeping pups.

'Of that I have little doubt,' was the reply. 'Yourself has the hunter's eye, Macfie. Which pup would you choose?'

Macfie looked again, and saw that they were of equal size, but one was brindled like the mother, the other blacker than the raven's wing. 'For my part I would choose the black,' he decided at length.

'Then it will travel with you on the morrow,' said the old woman. 'Treat it well, Macfie. Be patient and forbearing with it always and the day will come when it will repay you with its life.'

Next day Macfie carried home with him the black pup. The woman would take no payment, but she repeated her wish that the animal be well cared for, and once more assured him that it would repay his kindness with its life. But though he tried repeatedly to return to the *bochan* hidden in the hills his searching was in vain. Nor was any woman answering to his description known throughout the island.

In time the black pup grew up and promised well, for it learned quickly, showed more than usual intelligence and possessed great strength and fleetness of foot. At last the day came when Macfie decided it was ready for the hunt.

'Tomorrow we will go to Jura,' he told his seven sons, 'and we will match the black hound with the red stags of that island.' The boat was made ready against the voyage, but when the time came for them to depart, the black hound stood stubbornly on the shore and would not enter the boat.

When they tried to force it aboard the galley it turned tail and ran to the hills. Macfie was disappointed, but he restrained his sons from hunting it down and chastising it. 'We will try the hound another day. It may be that it is afraid of the sea.'

But though Macfie went many times with his sons to Jura, not once would the hound accompany them even to the shore. 'The hound is useless, fit meat for the hoody crows,' scoffed the young men, who by this time would have slain it without hesitation.

But as before Macfie stayed them. 'His day will surely come,' he told them, remembering the words of the mysterious old woman.

One day they prepared to return for the last time that season to Jura. 'What of the black hound!' joked the young men. 'Where will it hide itself today?' Macfie made no reply, for as usual the hound had taken himself elsewhere. But on their way to launch the galley, great was their astonishment. The black hound leapt before them across the sand and sprang aboard the galley without bidding.

Thereafter the voyage was made beneath a cloudless sky, and the galley sped before a steady wind. The black hound was first to reach the shores of Jura, and could scarcely be curbed as the hunters climbed towards the deer forests, Then, at the first corrie in the hills, it halted and refused to lead or follow. As before it resisted capture, and Macfie was forced to leave the sullen creature to skulk amongst the crags.

But before the party reached the first summit a change of weather threatened. Black clouds rolled up from the west, and a gale struck the island. The darkness fell so suddenly that Macfie and his sons made haste to return to the boat. But the fury of wind and rain drove them to shelter in a cave, and there they waited while thunder rolled from hill to hill, and the fierce gale plucked the heather from the slopes and tossed it into the darkness.

At last sleep came to the hunters one by one, until Macfie alone was left to listen to the howling of the wind, his eyes ever on the mouth of the cave. It seemed to him that he saw a shadow enter, and he felt a warm heavy body lay itself at his feet. The black hound had returned. The storm increased in fury. Macfie shivered in the darkness for now it seemed that the powers of evil had followed the black- hound, and were gathering about him in the cave. The hound too was restless, stirring every now and then and growling in its throat.

Suddenly a hand touched Macfie and closed about his neck. He started up but was at once flung against the wall of the cavern. At that moment the black hound sprang to the attack and grappled with the unseen enemy. Macfie cowered while the conflict continued, deafened by the howls of anguish and fury that echoed from wall to wall, calling for his sons to rise. At length the combatants were locked across his body; the breath was driven from him and he fell back unconscious. No more did he know until he awoke in the grey light of daybreak.

He looked about him. His seven sons lay as if in sleep, but each of them was dead. Across his feet was spread the broken body of the black hound, its teeth holding a bloodstained hand and arm wrenched from some gigantic body. At that his reason left him and he fled the cave.

Macfie returned to Colonsay with his story that is talked of yet. Within a month he had grown an old and feeble man, but he would not rest until he returned with retainers to the cave on Jura. The bodies of his seven sons had vanished, as had the great hand and arm. And when it seemed that the tale he had told was no more than his imaginings, the islanders saw in a cleft of rock the body of the black hound. And the horror of its shape and the scars of burning everywhere convinced them that it had fought with something beyond the ken of mortal man.

Tir-nan-og

Aodh, son of Aodh, fisherman of Isle Oronsay, was out in the bay in his own small coracle, drifting in the slack water. Sometimes he fished for the flat-fish lurking in the sand in the shallow water, and sometimes he lay in the stern doing nothing at all.

The summer heat had gone from the sun, for the season was nearly spent. Already the hand of autumn was laid upon the land, bleaching the seagrass and spreading gold and russet and earth-brown across the moor and the gentle uplands. Aodh loved the bay of golden sand where the little ducks came in winter, but better still he loved the little outer isles and their narrow creeks where the shoals of white fish gathered.

Yard by yard the coracle drifted towards the sandbars, out into the blue open water where the seals played. Aodh decided he would put about before meeting the full blast of the wind. But when he plied the oars he knew he had been foolish. A sudden squall swung the vessel into the current. It began to drift seawards on a course of its own.

No-one saw Aodh leave the bay, to vanish round the last headland. By nightfall the hills of home had gone, the night clouds had lowered, and the frail coracle tossed helplessly before the rising wind. When it seemed that the waves must bring about disaster, a flock of oyster-catchers flew out of the darkness to circle the coracle. Where they flew the sea became calm and the wind had no power upon the waves.

The birds remained until the dawn broke. A green isle appeared upon the horizon, and to it the birds flew swiftly, leaving Aodh to bring the coracle into calm water, without shoal or ripple. He dragged it high up a smooth strand. But the sudden uncanny stillness roused in him a little fear that he had sailed beyond the world, and made him plunge his knife into a hillock as he had been told to do. For the wise fishermen said that to do this would drive away the powers of evil.

Suddenly he heard someone singing in a sweet voice. He followed the sound and saw a maiden seated on a rock. Tall she was, and slender as the birch-tree. Her golden hair fell on white shoulders, and her face was lovelier than that of any maiden he had ever known. She called him to her side, and as he sat at her feet he knew he would love her for ever.

The years passed. Each day that dawned upon the green isle increased his love for the maiden. Never had he known such happiness. The sun had never shone so brightly. It was indeed a place of everlasting peace, without shadow of unhappiness. But the day came when Aodh began to dream of Isle Oronsay. He tried to put the thoughts from him, but each day they returned more urgently, in the end leading him back to the shore where his coracle lay above the gentle tide.

At length he decided to sail again to the land he had almost forgotten. When he told the maiden of his longing she grew sad.

'That cannot be, Aodh, son of Aodh. Seven years you have lived on Tir-nan-og, the Land of the Ever Young, from which there is no return.'

'My coracle is sound, and still will float,' he replied.

'No farther than a span from the shore, beloved, Then return it must - or sink beneath the bed of the sea.'

Then Aodh realised that for all its beauty this isle of everlasting youth was no more than a prison holding them both captive. But he did not tell her of the dagger thrust in the little hill by the shore that would still let him go free.

In the morning she followed him to the beach. 'Come with me as far as the point yonder,' he said as he set the coracle in the water.

'There and no farther can either of us go,' she replied as she stepped into the craft.

But when he reached the point of land he turned the bow seawards, riding the waves steadily into the east.

But no sooner had they reached the open sea than a change came upon the maiden. Aodh found her weeping in the stern, and with each tear that fell it seemed a little of her beauty faded.

For three days and three nights they sailed on a troubled sea. Then with the fourth dawn the outline of Isle Oronsay appeared on the horizon. Aodh steered the coracle into the safety of the bay he knew so well.

Aodh leapt ashore and turned towards the maiden. 'Come now, best-beloved,' he cried happily. 'Come with me to my own house upon the hill, where no evil spell can befall us.'

The maiden made no reply. He called her again. She cowered against the rocks, with her head turned to where the gulls were wheeling and the oyster-catchers piped on the far rocks, her shawl gathered close about her. He called her a third time, approaching to pull aside the shawl as he lifted her lightly in his arms. When at last she turned he no longer saw the form and face of a young and beautiful maiden, but the shrivelled features and crooked body of an ancient crone.

'O Aodh, son of Aodh!' she wept in sorrow, 'let us return to the green isle where I may find my youth again and keep it for ever!'

With a heavy heart Aodh realised that the old tales were true. Those who returned from the enchanted isle forfeited not only youth and beauty but happiness. He took his loved one by the hand, turned his back on Isle Oronsay for ever, and together they put to sea to seek the Land of Lost Content.

Sometimes the fishermen of the isles tell a tale of how a lonely coracle appears upon the horizon, on its endless search for Tir-nan-og, the Land of the Ever Young. But always the wind comes and it vanishes as mysteriously as it appears. When it happens they look to their sheets, for they have come to know that surely a storm is on its way.

PART TWO *by Alisdair Alpin McGregor*

Faery folk and their secrets

It may not be known generally that Highland and Hebridean faeries live lives not very dissimilar to those of ordinary mortals, have many of the same pleasures, fears and inhibitions, are practised in many of the same handicrafts, possess livestock, maintain arms for offensive and defensive purposes, are liable to fall victim to the same diseases, and require food, shelter and clothing.

Ordinary humans, who at one time or another have been privileged to visit Faeryland, have assured us on their return that the faeries are engaged in occupation identical with those associated with human activity. Many members of the fraternity, for example, are blacksmiths, and work laboriously at the making of agricultural implements, and of such weapons as faery arrows.

They eat, they dance, they make merry. When they are tired, they fall asleep in the ordinary way. Their women-folk spin and weave, milk and churn, grind the grain with querns, cook the food, bake bread, and even sing at their work. When commodities run short, or when they require the use of a utensil which they may not possess, they borrow the same from their faery neighbours, just as do many classes of mankind.

Their dwellings are underground, and are lit by lights in everyday use; and their tables are often adorned with vessels of silver and gold. All things about their homes are lustrous and gorgeous. Their clothing, as a rule, is extravagant.

Their diet is rich and varied. It consists chiefly of articles meant for human consumption, out of which the faery folk take the *toradh* or substance, leaving for mankind merely the bulk without any food value at all. In addition to the food they acquire from men, they feed on such viands as *brisgean*, the root of the silver-weed, which is ploughed up in great quantities in spring-time, and in olden days was known as the Seventh Bread. They also have a partiality for the stalks and tops of heather, and for young, fresh heather-shoots. Their milk is the milk of the goat and of the red deer hind; and the milk of ordinary cows spilt in the byre, or between the byre and the house, has been regarded as their perquisite through many centuries. The elle-woman, or female faery, often may be seen on the hills, milking the hinds, just as ordinary, mortal women milk domesticated cows.

Close to the knolls or knowes, which form the faeries' habitations, and are sometimes spoken of as Elf-hillocks, may be found those circles of dark-green grass, known as Faery Rings, or Faery Greens. On these the faeries dance and revel when, on moonlit nights, they emerge from their dwellings underground. Under no circumstances must mortal men essary to cultivate a Faery Green, or permit their livestock to damage or pollute it in any way. Murrain among beasts - the fifth of the dreaded plagues of Egypt in the days of Moses - befell the cattle of a crofter in Caithness who interfered with a faery knowe; and so serious was the plague that the need-fire had to be employed to stay it. The need-fire, or neid-fire, was the name applied to fire produced by the friction of two pieces of wood. To such fire certain virtues were superstitiously attached in olden times.

The following quotation from Chamber's *Popular Rhymes* describes what may happen when one seeks to till a Faery Green:

> *'He wha tills the faeries' green*
> *Nae luck again shall hae:*
> *And he wha spills the faeries' ring*
> *Betide him want and wae,*
> *For weirdless days and weary nights*
> *Are his till his deein' day.*
> *But he wha gaes by the faery ring,*
> *Nae dule nor pine shall see;*
> *And he wha cleans the faery ring,*
> *An easy death shall dee.'*

Faeryland is ruled by a king - the King of the Faeries. He is assisted in the administration of his court and kingdom by his wife, who is designated the Queen of the Faeries, or the Queen of Elfin. The prevalence of this belief is shown by all manner of documentary evidence.

Among the admissions of the Auldearn witches, when on trial in 1662, is that of Isobel Gowdie. 'I was in Downie Hills,' Isobel confessed, 'and got meat there from the Queen of the Fairies, more than I could eat. The queen is brawly clothed in white linen, and in white and brown cloth: the king is a braw man, well favoured and broad-faced. There were plenty of elf bulls rowting (bellowing) and skoyling (squealing) up and down, and affrighted me.'

It is said that faeries always come from the west, and that they are able to enter houses, however well protected such houses may be against their invasion. All manner of devices were resorted to in former times - aye, and even at the present day in certain parts of the Highlands and Islands - to counteract their activities. Cattle killed by accidentally falling over cliffs are looked upon as being especially liable to faery influence; and thus a nail was driven into such a victim as soon after the accident as possible, in order to keep the faery folk away from the carcass.

The bannock made with the last pickle of meal at the end of the baking also kept them away, but only when a hole had been pierced in it by the finger, or when it had been placed under a fragment of burning fuel. It was customary, also, to remove the band from the spinning-wheel at bed-time, particularly on Saturday nights, for otherwise the faeries invaded the house and used the wheel after its inmates had retired for the night. The hum of the spinning-wheel frequently was heard during the night in houses where, inadvertently, the band had been left on the wheel; but in the morning no evidences of spinning could be seen anywhere, and the wheel itself was often found in a damaged condition.

In Ireland it was usual to remove the band from the wheel in order to frustrate the faeries' predisposition for spoiling the linen. Then, the last handful of grain reaped at the end of the harvest was made up into what was known as the Harvest Maiden. This figure was suspended somewhere in the farmer's house, to act as a protection against the faeries' wiles until the following harvest, when it was replaced by a new one.

By the same token, sprigs of holly were used for decorative purposes on the last day of the year. And one reason why water-stoups were filled at night and brought into the house was that the faeries might have plenty of liquid with which to slake their thirst, without their having to seek other sources of liquid at the expense of mankind.

Both the Women of Peace, as female faeries were called, and their masculine counterpart, the Men of Peace, according to tradition, lured members of the human race into their subterranean retreats, and regaled them sumptuously. Both, likewise, wore green garments, and were believed to take a spite against ordinary mortals who presumed to wear their colour. Dundee's misfortune at Killiecrankie was attributed by the Highlanders to his having been dressed in green on that fateful occasion. To this day many of the name of Graham regard this colour as being of evil omen; and on no account will they wear it.

The faeries, moreover, tempted mortals to partake of their food, and to join in their merriment. When ordinary mortals did so, they forfeited their power to remain members of human society, and were tied down irrevocably to observing the constitution governing the affairs of the Men of Peace.

The story is told of a woman who was transported into the secret recesses of the Men of Peace, where she was recognised by one of their number, who claimed to have known her when he himself was an ordinary mortal. This faery apparently retained a modicum of benevolence, since he counselled her to abstain from eating and drinking with them for a definite space of time during her retention in faeryland, if she desired her freedom. This advice she took. Thus, when the assigned period had elapsed, she was restored to the society of mortals. The tradition continues that, when afterwards she came to examine the food offered her by the Men of Peace, she found it to consist "only of the refuse of the earth."

From all accounts, the faeries dwelling in the Highlands were not so brazen as their kinsfolk inhabiting the Shetland Isles, since the latter appear to have had no qualms about carrying off young children, even after they had been baptised, meanwhile seeing to it that in their place they substituted something in the nature of a cabbage stalk or two, which they altered into the appearance of the abducted infant. The bereft mother in such circumstances was obliged to bestow upon the substitute the same care and attention as that which she would have bestowed upon her own child. It was firmly believed in the Shetlands that, if she acted otherwise towards the substitute, the Men of Peace would deprive her finally of her child.

Said a Shetland mother to a neighbour, who was condoling with her because of the wasted appearance of the infant on her knee: 'This is not my bairn. May the devil rest where my bairn is now!'

The following folk-tales, selected from many that have come my way in recent years, are illustrative of faery life and habit.

Captured

Not so long ago, a woman and her infant son, living at Rahoy, in the Morven district of Argyll, were transported mysteriously to Ben Iadain, a hill in the neighbourhood reputed to have been the domicile of faeries.

As the woman herself afterwards explained, they were taken to the

Black Door, that being the name then given to the faeries' main entrance to the interior of the hill. Within the hill they encountered a vast throng of people of all ages, among whom was a young lad who approached the woman and bade her not to refuse such food as the faeries might offer her but to take it and conceal it in her clothing.

He explained to her that he and his mother had been carried hither in like manner and that neither of them could get away because of his mother's indiscretion in having partaken of the faeries' food, and her bidding him to do likewise.

When the faery-in-chief learnt that the woman refused to consume any of the food supplied to her, he sent a band of his henchmen to bring in a certain man's cow. But they returned without the cow, explaining that they could not touch it since its right knee was resting on the plant known as the dirk grass. He then sent them forth for another cow; but they came back with the news that the milk-maid, on her own confession, had just put an iron shackle on it. A third time the faery henchmen sallied forth for yet another cow; but they learnt to their dismay that this cow had just consumed a quantity of the magical plant called the *mothan*.

That night the woman's husband had a dream, in which the whereabouts of his wife and child were revealed, and in which he was instructed to tie three knots in the silk kerchief his wife wore at her marriage, and take it to the Black Door. Thus equipped, the husband entered the interior of Ben Iadain, and rescued his wife and infant son.

As for the lad, who had warned the woman not to consume any of the food offered her by her captors, he still may be held captive by the faeries, for all we know!

Phantom troops & a mystery flag

At Dunvegan Castle, in the Isle of Skye, may be seen the famous Faery Flag, one of the most fascinating relics of Faerie in the country. According to one version of its origin, we are told that late on an autumn evening a faery, clad in green, entered the Castle and found her way to what since has been termed the Faery Room. There she discovered the baby heir to MacLeod, asleep in his cradle.

You may imagine how surprised MacLeod's nurse was when she looked up to find a strange little woman seated beside the cradle, rocking it gently. The faery visitor raised the child in her arms, and wrapped him up in the Faery Flag, crooning the while the *Taladh na Mna Sithe*, the Lullaby of the Faery Woman - 'Behold my child, limbed like the kid or fawn, smiting horses, grasping the accoutrements of the shod horses, the spirited steeds, *mo leanabh bheag*, my little child... Oh! that I could behold thy team of horses; men following them, serving women returning home, and the Catanaich sowing the corn... Oh! not of Clan Kenneth (MacKenzie) art thou! Oh! not of Clan Conn. Descendant of a race more esteemed - that of Clan Leod of the swords and armour, whose fathers' native land was Lochlann.' Thus runs an extract from a free translation of the faery woman's croon made by my late and venerated friend, Francis Tolmie.

Spellbound and motionless during the singing of it sat the nurse of the infant heir; and so impressed upon her memory was the croon that she forgot neither its words nor its melody. When the faery woman disappeared, the nurse lifted the child from his cot wherein he had been replaced; and, having hurried with him down the stair that still winds in the Faery Tower of Dunvegan, carried him into the banqueting-hall, where, in splendour and elegance, were assembled many members of the Clan. And great, to be sure, was their consternation when they cast eyes upon the magic banner, and listened to the strange story that the nurse had to tell.

For a long, long time the MacLeods of Dunvegan insisted that every nurse should be able to sing the Croon of the Faery Woman, because they firmly believed it acted as a *seun* or charm that would protect the infant chieftains from all manner of evil.

In these times the Faery Flag was committed to the charge of a family whose head acted as hereditary custodian of it, and bore it into battle whenever the occasion demanded. MacLeod maintained his **duin'-bratach** or standard-bearer on a freehold near Bracadale, in return for his services in this connection.

But the more generally accepted theory of the Faery Flag is that it came into the possession of a young MacLeod warrior during his absence in the Land of the Infidel. This crusader was none other than Mac a' Phearsan - to wit, the Son of the Parson. During his wanderings in the Holy Land, this knight-errant came to a broad river, where he met the *maighdean-sith* - the faery maiden - who would not permit him to cross until he had wrestled with her as Jacob wrestled with the angel at Penuel.

In the legendary struggle that ensued, the MacLeod warrior overcame his elfin adversary; and, while departing from her, he was presented with the Faery Flag that she assured him, when unfurled, would give the appearance of a great multitude of armed men. Be it said, moreover, that the faery maiden warned the crusader only to use the banner on three specific occasions, and told him that, among other calamities, the misuse of it would result in there being no young cattle nor sheep in the territory of the MacLeods. No cow would have a calf; and, likewise, every mare and ewe would become sterile. Furthermore, there would be plenteousness neither of crops nor of fish for a whole year: nor would any children be born unto MacLeod.

A third version states that one of the chiefs of MacLeod was betrothed to a faery, who dwelt on earth with him only for a short space of time, and that, when she was bidding him farewell before her return to faery-land, she presented him with the Faery Flag as a keepsake. The actual spot where the chief and the faery finally took leave of one another is about three miles from Dunvegan. It is still known as the Faery Bridge (*Drochaid nan tri Allt*, the Bridge of the Brooks), and is situated just at the point where the Portree, Dunvegan, and Vaternish roads converge.

Magic millers

Long ago the parish minister of Tiree employed a manservant who, to his dying day, avowed that when bringing a cartload of meal home one night from the island mill, he heard quern-stones operating in the centre of the Red Knowes, by the roadside.

He stopped the horse and cart to listen for a while. The sound of the querns continued unceasingly; and from this the minister's manservant concluded that the faeries must have had a considerable quantity of grain in their subterranean granary.

All attempts to dispel what many of his neighbours regarded as a delusion failed completely. Neither minister nor kirk-session could disabuse his mind of belief in faeries, and of the faeries' ability to grind corn with the quern, for he insisted that he had listened to this faery milling 'with my own ears!'

Faery music

According to some, who claim to be authorities on matters faerie, the bagpipes are the only musical instrument known to the faeries of the Highlands and Islands; and it is believed that in olden times many of the most celebrated pipers in Scotland learnt their art originally from the Little People.

Occasionally, however, we hear of the proficiency with which certain faery folks are able to play the *clarsach*, or Celtic harp. I know two or three people among my own acquaintances who have listened to faery harping, and who can remember fragments of the melodies they heard.

A faery orchestra

There is a tale told in the Lewis of how two young men chanced to be passing a faery knoll at the witching hour, when the knoll suddenly opened and emitted a green light. For a moment the men stood in astonishment, not knowing what had befallen them, until they realised that they were listening to a faery orchestra secreted in the very interior of the knoll.

So overcome was one of them by the strains of faery music - he himself being a fiddler of sorts - that he straightway forsook his companion, and made for the green light. No sooner had the passing fiddler been admitted to the company of the faeries than the knoll closed. And so enchanted was he by the music of the faery orchestra, and he himself contributing his part with a fiddle the faeries had lent him, that he eventually returned to his people in the belief that he had been absent but a few hours, whereas he actually had been away a year and a day.

So well did he play his fiddle thereafter that no one dared disbelieve his story that he had performed with a faery orchestra. Music equally enthralling was once heard by a Skye-man in the Braes of Portree, when passing the hillock known to the Gaelic-speaking natives by a name signifying Faery Knowe of the Beautiful Mountain.

And, then, delightful pipe-music has been heard issuing from underneath the Dun of Caolis, at the eastern end of Tiree; and the old folks of Tiree used to say that to this music they often heard the marching of many feet underground.

The Brownie

Folk tales relating to the supernatural creature called the Brownie are almost as common throughout the Highlands and Islands of Scotland as are faery-tales. Several ancient and well-known Highland homes are said to have housed a Brownie, although in Scotland, as elsewhere, belief in the existence of Brownies is much more recent than faith in the existence of the Faery Folk.

Opinions vary as to the physical proportions of the average Brownie, and as to his general appearance. According to Thomas Pennant, he was stout and blooming, carried a fine head of flowing hair, and moved noiselessly from place to place with a switch in his hand. Other authorities describe him as having been short in stature, curly-headed, and wrinkle-faced. But many depict him in a much more attractive form. Be this as it may, the Highland Brownie has always been regarded with esteem and affection.

Generally speaking, Brownies were said to take up residence in the castles and mansions of the more affluent families; and, even when such abodes fell into desuetude and ultimate decay, Brownies have been known to stay on among the ruins for considerable periods. Several of them are believed to have lived to a great age. For example, the Brownie that haunted the corridors of Leithin Hall, in Dumfriesshire, is reputed to have remained there continuously throughout three centuries.

That the Brownie took upon himself social and domestic duties which were varied, and usually of a beneficent character, is amply illustrated by the following folk tales relating to distinguished members of this elfin brotherhood.

The Little Old Man of the Barn

Up till the time of 'the Forty-five,' it is said, every clachan and farm in the Highlands of Perthshire had its own Brownie. This beneficent fellow went by a Gaelic name signifying the Little Old Man of the Barn, since he used to assist in threshing the corn with the flail, and in redding up the barn by gathering up the straw into tidy sheaves for the bedding of the livestock.

The barn he looked upon as his special province. Brownies with duties such as these got their name because of their wisdom and elderly appearance. The activities of the Little Old Man of the Barn were confined to the night-time. All his threshing was done after midnight; and it was his plan to see that he had quitted the binding of the sheaves were any human being astir.

> *'Whan thair wes come to thrashe or dichte,*
> *Or Barne or byre to clene,*
> *He had ane bizzy houre at nichte,*
> *Atween the twall and ane."*

The Little Old Man of the Barn had an equivalent on the Isle of Man in the person of the Grey-headed One (*Glaisein*), who paid periodic visits to farms, threshed corn, and attended the fold.

A Colonsay Brownie

Colonsay also had its Brownie, upon whom devolved somewhat similar duties; and there are folks still living at Uragaig, on that Island, who remember clearly when elderly natives used to pour into a cavity in the ground a libation of milk for the sustenance of this creature, in order to ensure the continuance of his good graces.

As recently as 1880 a Colonsay woman admitted to Symington Grieve, author of that exhaustive work, *The Book of Colonsay & Oronsay*, that she sometimes poured milk into a basin for the supernatural creature called the glaistig. Belief in Brownies and glaistigs persisted in Colonsay right down to the present century. As recently as May 1910, crofters placed milk in the cavity of a stone near Balnahard farmhouse. This was done each year, and on the first night on which the cattle were left out all night. On such occasions each crofter was obliged to give the whole of the night's milk from one cow. Once he had poured this milk into the cavity, it became incumbent upon him to turn away immediately, and not look back under any circumstances.

The invisible herdsman

Brownies are also known to have taken upon themselves the duties of the herdsman. When, as in olden times, arable land was tilled and reaped in common throughout the Isles, difficulty was often experienced, especially during the night-time, in keeping the cows away from the crops.

There is a tradition in the Island of Tiree, however, that the crofters at the township of Baugh were relieved of this irksome responsibility by the constant services of a Brownie who, in an invisible capacity, acted as herdsman between the hours of sunset and sunrise.

No ordinary person ever cast eyes on this Brownie, though many a vigil was instituted in the expectation of ascertaining what he was like, and whence he came. One endowed with the second-sight stayed out all night with the cattle; and he declared in the morning that he actually saw an impalpable creature herding the cattle down to the machar by the shore when it looked as though they were beginning to graze too near the crops. This he took to be the Brownie herdsman, of whose existence everyone had heard. The Brownie wore little or no clothing. This moved the observer to pity - so much so, indeed, that he offered the Brownie a pair of shoes and a pair of tiny breeks. It was then that the Brownie divulged his name, as he declined the offer with:

> *'Shoes and breeks on Gunna,*
> *And Gunna at the herding;*
> *But may Gunna enjoy neither shoes nor breeks,*
> *If he should herd the cattle any more."*

With these words the Invisible Herdsman took his departure; and ever since that incident the folks of Tiree have been obliged to do their own herding of nights.

The Cara Brownie

A little to the south of Gigha, an island some little distance off the western shore of Kintyre, lies the islet of Cara. On this islet once stood an ancient house that belonged to the MacDonalds of Largie; and in that house there resided a Brownie, the special guardian of the family and its fortunes.

Like all other creatures of his kind, the Cara Brownie subsisted largely, if not entirely, on milk and cream. Unlike his kindred, however, he had a great ill-will at the Campbells. In pristine days, when the MacDonalds inhabited the old Castle of Largie, situated above the Kintyre shore, there was a Brownie that showed great affection for the family; and it is commonly believed in Argyll that, when Largie Castle was deserted for Cara, the Brownie flitted thither with the rest of the household.

The particular function of the Cara Brownie was to make preparations for the arrival of strangers or guests. He aired the beds, and changed the bed-linen when necessary: he saw to it that no dirty dishes nor clothes were left unattended to overnight: at bed-time he took upon himself the responsibility for seeing that all the dogs were out of the house, and tied up at their respective kennels. He stumbled purposely over the water-stoups lying about during the night, as a hint to those who carelessly had left them. And he had a habit of giving a sharp skelp in the dark to any inmate guilty of dirtiness or untidiness about the house. Indeed, it is less than half a century since persons were alive in Argyll who deponed to their having received a flick or two at the hands of the meticulous Brownie.

On one occasion a man was taken out of his bed, and did not realise it until he woke to find himself standing stark naked before the smouldering fire. On another occasion a herdswoman, delayed one evening in setting out to bring the cows home, could not locate them. When she returned to the steading, she found them duly tied up in the byre. For both of these strange happenings the Brownie of Cara was deemed responsible.

This Brownie, it is said, has neither been seen nor heard on the mainland of Kintyre since the modern residence was built. But he is still heard on the islet of Cara.

The water-horse

Although today belief in the existence of the *each uisge*, or water-horse, seems to have disappeared completely, it is only the matter of a few decades since every locality of the Highlands and Islands was reputed to possess a loch haunted by such a creature. The prevalence of this belief is attested by the number and variety of the folk tales still told of the water-horse and its sinister activities. There is scarcely a district of Celtic Scotland that does not have its water-horse tradition.

Similarly, belief in the existence of the *tarbh uisge*, or water-bull, has waned, though at no time did this creature occupy so much of the attention of the natives as did the water-horse. The idea that lochs, such as Loch Hourn and Loch Awe, were the abode of some fearsome creature of monstrous dimensions has been revived in our own time by the recent graphic descriptions given by independent eye-witnesses of the world-famous Loch Ness Monster.

Shieling of the One Night

In a fertile glen not far distant from the village of Shawbost, in the west of Lewis, there lies a shieling that for more than a century has gone by a Gaelic name meaning the Shieling of the One Night. This shieling was started by a couple of families who agreed to sharing equally their rights in it.

One evening in June, just at the commencement of shieling-time, two cousins in their early twenties, known locally as Fair Mary and Dark Mary, occupied the shieling for the first time since its erection. Having milked their cows and put in a spell at the churning, they sat in the low doorway of their summer dwelling, singing and knitting until the hour for retiring.

As they were putting a light on the cruisie, there came to the shieling a woman, of whom they had no acquaintance. She professed weariness of body and mind, and asked a night's hospitality. There seemed nothing unusual about her mein, since she was clad in the customary dress of the Lewis peasant woman, and spoke with such intimacy of the neighbouring countryside that the two Marys saw no reason to deny her the traditional hospitality of the Isles.

Now, as a rule, two-thirds of the interior of a shieling are occupied by a bed, which generally consists of a shake-down of straw or of heather. After a simple repast, the Marys and their guest retired for the night. At dawn of day, however, Dark Mary awoke with a fright, and felt a warm trickle by her side. Up she leapt in great horror to discover the guest gone, and a stream of blood flowing from the breast of her cousin, who now was dead.

On forcing open the rude doorway of the shieling, she noticed a horse trotting away and away toward the greying of the day. No explanation seemed necessary now. The horse was nothing more or less than the dreaded *each uisge*, or water-horse, to which she and her dead cousin, Fair Mary, had unwittingly offered hospitality the previous evening, believing her to have been a woman, footsore, and genuinely seeking a night's portion.

The corpse of the water-horse's victim, they say in Lewis, was interred on the slope to the east of this shieling of unhappy memory, the tumble-down shell of which is still to be seen. Never since has this shieling been occupied. Hence the ominous name by which it is known to this day - Shieling of the One Night.

The white horse of Spey

Perhaps the most fitful and unreliable of all our Scottish rivers is the Spey. Its floods and spates are proverbial; and historical records of the destruction they have wrought to life and property show that there is a touch of modesty in the old saying that computes the Spey's demand at one life a year.

In this respect, however, the Spey is regarded as being less rapacious than the Dee -

> *'Ravenous Dee*
> *Yearly takes three!'*

Among the folks of Spey-side there was an ancient belief that the loss of life by drowning in that river was due to the alluring machinations of the White Horse of Spey, a creature described by them as a beautiful beast to the sight, but in reality a kelpie of ill-doing. Seldom during good weather was the White Horse seen, or was there any evidence of its evil existence.

But on boisterous nights, when thunders pealed among the Cairngorms and the Hills of Cromdale, his whinnying was often heard, and his form almost as frequently seen.

And it was his custom in circumstance of storm, they say, to accost benighted pedestrians and assure them of safe escort to their destination. By the side of the footsore wanderer he would walk, until the former became so overcome with fatigue as to accept gladly the offer of being conveyed astraddle for the remainder of his journey. Once a-mount the White Horse of Spey, the rider's fate was sure, for the fearsome creature then galloped off at break-neck pace, and plunged into the deep pools of the Spey, carrying with him the rider who, by some power of magic, remained fixed immovably to its back.

Tradition in Spey-side has it that the White Horse claimed innumerable victims in this way; and of the exultant song sung by the White Horse, in his death-dash, the following fragment has been handed down to us:

> *'And ride weel, Davie,*
> *And by this night at ten o'clock*
> *Ye'll be in Pot Cravie,'*

In her charming book, *The Secret of Spey*, Wendy Wood gives another fragment of the White Horse's song, which she picked up locally:

> *'Ride you; Ride me,*
> *Kelpie, Creavie!"*

Yet another version of the kelpie's song is given by a Cairney contributor to the official journal of the Banff Field Club in 1884. 'I remember, when children,' writes this contributor, 'we used to be told that the water-kelpie would sing to the poor, deluded ones he managed to entice away:

> *'Sit weel, Janety, or ride weel, Davie,*
> *For this time the morn ye'll be in Pot Cravie.' '*

The black steed of Loch Pityoulish

Reminiscent of the White Horse of Spey is the story of the black steed of Loch Pityoulish, a picturesque loch situated between the Spey and the foothills of the Cairngorms. Local tradition is insistent that the loch harbours some dreaded monster, and that no-one bathing in its water should ever allow his head to become submerged. This tradition may have emanated from the sunken crannog or lake-dwelling of pre-historic times, the site of which one may see on a calm, clear day, deep down below the surface of the loch.

In any case, the inhabitants of Kincardine regarded the crannog as a submerged castle; and with it they associated all sorts of queer and eerie beliefs.

On a day when the heir to the Barony of Kincardine was playing with his young friends by the shore of Loch Pityoulish, their attention was drawn to a beautiful steed grazing near at hand, harnessed with a silver saddle, silver bridle and silver reins. In great excitement all the boys grasped the reins, whereat the black steed galloped off into the loch, dragging them with him. Only the heir to the Barony came home to tell the tale, since, as it happened, he was able to free himself by severing his rein-fast fingers with a knife he carried. Since that day the folks of Kincardine have been wary of the water-horse inhabiting the sunken crannog in Loch Pityoulish.

Evil at Loch nan Dubhrachan

Perhaps the most memorable incident connected with the water-horse in the Highlands of Scotland was the dragging of a loch in Skye with a view to capturing this evil monster.

Between Knock and Isle Oronsay, in the Sleat of Skye, is a loch called Loch nan Dubhrachan. So persistent in the neighbourhood were stories of the manner in which 'a beast' inhabiting this loch sought to waylay islanders who dared to pass by at night-time, that eventually it was decided to drag the loch with a large net. This was actually carried out in the year 1870. But the animal astutely evaded capture. During the dragging operations, however, the net became entangled with some object under water. This so terrified both spectators and those engaged in dragging the net on opposite sides of the loch that they all fled to their homes, convinced that at long last they had proved the existence of the water-horse.

In 1932 I visited an old man named John MacRae, who lived in a cottage by the steading, within earshot of the Old Manse of Glen Elg, and who, as a boy at Isle Oronsay, witnessed the attempt to capture this water-horse. So noisy in spate was the burn at the end of John MacRae's cottage that at times I used to find conversation with him quite an undertaking, even when the door was closed. But I managed to take down from him a most interesting verbatim account of the dragging of Loch nan Dubhrachan.

The dragging of Loch nan Dubhrachan recalls a traditional attempt to drain a 'bottomless' loch situated in the neighbourhood of Tomintoul, in the uplands of Banff. This loch was haunted by a kelpie, who was believed to have been responsible for the mysterious disappearance from early times of innumerable persons. When the men of Strathdon assembled, and commenced to drain the water away, a terrifying shriek came from the depths of the loch, and a little man, with a flaming red bonnet on his head, made his appearance. The men of Strathdon immediately fled in panic, leaving their implements behind them.

The monster of Loch Hourn

To this day the folks residing about Loch Hourn believe that loch to be haunted by a monster, to which they refer as the Wild Beast of Barrisdale.

Less than sixty years ago there lived at Barrisdale, by the shores of Loch Hourn, a crofter who once encountered this monster. He assured his neighbours that this ungainly creature had gigantic wings, and was three-legged. He often saw it in flight across the hills of Knoydart, especially about Barrisdale itself; and he averred that on one occasion, when it was making for him with evil design, he rushed for the shelter of his cottage. As the crofter himself used to relate up until the time of his death, he just succeeded in slamming the door in the monster's face.

The dwellers by the more remote shores of Loch Hourn frequently heard the terrifying roar of the Wild Beast of Barrisdale; and an old man living in this locality, called Ranald MacMaster, oft-times discovered the tracks of this three-legged creature on the hills, and also about the sandy stretches fringing Barrisdale Bay.

Beast of the Charred Forests

Hundreds and hundreds of years ago most of the Northern Highlands
and the Outer Hebrides was impenetrable forest. Tradition has it that,
in order to monopolise the timber trade, the Scandinavians fired the
woods of the Outer Hebrides. And, again, it is said that, with a view to
reducing the likelihood of their being set upon by the natives lying in
ambush, the Norsemen burned the woods, that they might be able to
observe any enemy advancing at a distance.

In Sutherland the destruction of the ancient forests is laid to the
charge of a fierce and powerful monster which roamed over the north of
Scotland, breathing fire wheresoever he went. As proof of this, the more elderly inhabitants point yet to the charred stumps of pine-trees embedded in
the peat-mosses. The entire populace fled for safety whenever the monster
was reported to be stalking the land. He came to be known among the folks
of Sutherland as the Beast of the Charred Forests.

'Pity on you, Dornoch!' roared the monster, as he came within sight
of the spire of St. Gilbert's Church.

'Pity on you, Dornoch!' repeated St. Gilbert, as he went forth to
meet the monster, armed with his bow and the sharpest of his arrows. With
the first arrow Gilbert pierced the hide of the monster, as he sought to
breathe fire upon Dornoch. Now, the townsfolk buried it under a large stone
situated on the moor between Dornoch and Skibo, and known traditionally
as the Beast's Stone. And, until a few years ago, it was quite usual for the
folks of this neighbourhood to compute local directions and distances in
relation to their being in such and such a direction and so many yards or
miles from the Beast's Stone.

Colann the Headless

The track of moorland about Morar known in olden times as the
Smooth Mile used to be haunted by a spectre called by the natives
Colann the Headless. This evil thing was wont to ensnare and destroy
the inhabitants at odd times as they passed along the Smooth Mile after
dark.

Efforts to rid the countryside of this menace involved the mysterious disappearance or death of all who made them. It was recognised that the strength of creatures such as Colann the Headless waned with the coming of daylight. And therefore Iain Garbh, one of the most doughty of the celebrated Chiefs of the MacLeods of Raasay, determined that he would try to overcome the spectre about the hour of dawn, since he was accustomed to pass this way when journeying between his island home and the south. However, long before dawn Iain Garbh and the headless one came to grips. With the coming of dawn its strength and prowess began to wane.

'Let me go!' entreated Colann, as the morning sun began to show above the hills of Morar.

'Not until thou swearest by the Book and the Seven Candles to quit this land forever,' rejoined MacLeod of Raasay.

Accordingly, Colann the Headless swore on oath; and he was released. Ever since that dawn on the Smooth Mile, Colann has confined himself to Beinn Eadarra, in the north of Skye; and to this very day the natives of Trotternish sing the song that he sang as he flew from the grips of Iain Garbh.

The sea-serpent

According to Highland and Island folklore, the largest creature in the world was the sea-serpent. This creature was known sometimes as the Great Whirlpool of the Ocean; and its internal capacity was defined in the old rhyme which said that it could contain in its belly no fewer than seven whales.

Mr Iain, a former minister of the Parish of Glen Elg, who died in 1875, was fond of sailing, and often put out to sea in his yacht. One day, while sailing with his two daughters, another clergyman, and a boy named Donald MacGrimmon, who assisted him with the sails, a huge monster rose quite close to the side of the yacht, putting such a wave aboard her that she was nearly swamped. The monster, my informant in Glen Elg assured me, 'was as big and as round as a herring barrel, and of great length. And it went wriggling up and down through the water, zigzag, right and left like.'

Greatly frightened, the occupants of the yacht kept on their course down toward the Sandaig Isles at the mouth of Loch Hourn. Meanwhile the monster, which they now realised was a sea-serpent, continued to disport itself dangerously close to the yacht. Once they had steered into Loch

Hourn, they saw it no more that day. They tarried some time at Arnisdale. When, on the morrow, they were about to return, one of Mr Iain's daughters insisted on being allowed to go home to the Manse of Glen Elg, on foot, a distance of thirteen miles, accompanied by a little terrier she had with her. The others returned by yacht; and again they encountered the sea-serpent at the mouth of Loch Hourn.

'In fact,' concluded my story-teller: 'they truly thought it had been waiting for them there. Och, I don't think it, though. Anyway, they got past it, and safely home after an exciting adventure!'

This no doubt, was the sea-serpent seen by an Islesman at Kylerhea some years ago. 'Yes, yes,' averred the Islesman in question, 'one day I saw the fearful head of the beast go down the Kyle; and, indeed, it was a week before his tail passed!'

By the roadside up near Scallasaig there is a serpent mound, where the people in olden times used to worship the serpent.

'How long ago would that be, John?' I asked the late John MacRae, aforementioned, a year or two before his death.

'Och, about two thousand years ago, I am sure,' responded John, now prepared to dilate considerably on the matter of serpents and serpent-mounds, and then I sat silently with my notebook and pencil, and wrote down the following as statement, word for word, from the lips of John MacRae:

'The mound was in the shape of a serpent; and when the chief of the people would die, he would be buried in the head of the serpent. One from London, that was going about searching things like that, opened the mound, and they found in the mound a big stone coffin with a big stone slab on the top. And there the bowl was found with the ashes of the chief of the people at that time. The bowl was taken to the Manse. That's about fifty years ago. It was there for a few months; and they took it to Edinburgh, to some museum or something. They were saying that there was a funny noise in the Manse when the bowl was lying there. If there was any treasure in the bowl, or in the grave along with the bowl it was taken out before. You see, had he any treasure - the chief like - guns and money and the like - I'm sure they wouldn't be putting much money in the grave. It would be going into the grave with the dead man, so, when he would rise in the next world, he would be ready to start at the same game as he was carrying on here on earth.'

A very bewildering statement, I grant you!

At Cosaig there is another serpent-mound. Some years ago the suggestion was made by a number of archaeologists that it also should be opened. Indeed, all the arrangements for the excavation of the site had been completed. But a violent thunderstorm broke the night before; and the people of Glen Elg were convinced that this storm was an expression of God's wrath at the proposed opening of the serpent-mound, which the natives regarded as an act of desecration. So great was the local pressure brought to bear on the archaeologists that finally the project was abandoned.

Raising the wind

In several of the Western Islands it was customary to resort to the well in order that favourable winds might be sent either to enable fishermen to reach the fishing-grounds, or to ensure the safe arrival of relatives coming by sea.

On the Isle of Gigha there is such a well. To it the MacNeils used to go when their galleys were wind-bound; and by stirring the water with a cane a favourable wind arose and conducted them whither they wished to sail. This particular well was called the *Tobar Mor*, the Great Well. It was covered over with a flat stone because the natives feared that one day it might flood the island. The captains of foreign vessels wind-bound in these waters used to give the natives a piece of money, in order that they might be permitted to consult the oracle as to the airt of the wind; and we read that all strangers were accustomed to leave at the well a coin or a pin as an oblation.

A spirit's reward

In a large island like Skye there are scores of wells, many of which have their own legendry. On the ancient beliefs connected with the wells of the Island of Skye alone a whole volume might be written.

When Martin Martin visited Loch Siant, in Skye, he found that the most celebrated well in the island was believed by the natives to be a specific against all distempers. The inhabitants, he tells us, obliged themselves by a vow to go to the well, and 'make the ordinary tour round it, called dessil, which is performed thus: They move thrice round the well, proceeding sunways from east to west, and so on. This is done after drinking of the

water; and when one goes away from the well, it is a never-failing custom
to leave some small offering on the stone which covers the well.'

Pilgrimages to this well were made till within comparatively recent
times. After a little ceremony had been observed, an offering was left for the
Spirit of the Well. A neighbouring loch and stream abounded with trout and
salmon; but no one would touch them, since they regarded them as sacred
fishes.

Water of life

**Nearby was another well esteemed by the people of Skye because its
water was reputed to remove all diseases instantly. The water of this
well was considered to be the lightest and 'wholesomest' in all the
Island. We are told that in time of war and scarcity the inhabitants were
able to subsist for many weeks by drinking the water of this well along
with fronds of dulse.**

Then, in the south of Skye, is the sacred well called by a Gaelic
name meaning the Well of the Trout. Centuries ago it contained a solitary
trout, which the islanders were exceedingly careful not to injure in any way.
Though they often caught the trout in their pails by mistake, they never
failed to replace it with extreme care.

Up from Glen Elg there is a well called *Tobar Bhan*, or the White
Well, from which a burn flows. In olden times the natives used to go to this
well to be cured of their ailments. Near the well they gathered water-cress,
and also the herb called 'flower of the three mountains,' for medicinal purposes. In this well there was once a sacred trout.

At Bernera, in Glen Elg, there is another well that likewise had a
trout in it. An old woman, Anne MacRae to name, used to clean this White
Well periodically, and sprinkle its approaches with gravel from the shore, so
as to keep it pure, and at the same time ensure the wellbeing of the sacred
trout. Anne had a great idea of the trout. But I was told in Glen Elg recently that the well contains no trout now, and that it disappeared about thirty-
three years ago with the death of Anne, its custodian.

Among the trees down by the Parish Church of Glen Elg, there is a
sacred well, known by a Gaelic name denoting the Well of Wine. It is three-
cornered, representing the Trinity, as do so many ancient wells.

The wells of St. Kilda

Among the wells and springs of St. Kilda, all of which deserve to be noted for their excellent water, is *Tobar nam Buaidh*, the Well of Virtues. This is the *Tou-bir-nimbeuy* of Martin, who writes of it as the finest of 'the excellent fountains or springs' in which St. Kilda abounds. The water of this well was considered efficacious against all manner of ailments. Referring to it in 1746, the Rev. Kenneth MacAulay notes that 'the water here was a sovereign cure for a great variety of distempers, deafness particularly, and every nervous disease.'

The Well of Virtues lies by the shieling in the Great Glen. On an altar hard by it, the islanders, who came to drink of it, were wont to leave offerings. So famed are its waters that for years the more nimble tourists, landing on St. Kilda from the Hebrides or the Dunara Castle, have dashed straight over the col between the Mullach Sgar and the Mullach Geal to drink of them during the few hours that either of these sister-ships may have been lying at anchor in Village Bay.

When in olden times the natives were delayed by contrary winds, they used to resort to *Tobar na Cille*, sometimes called the Well of St. Brendan. It is said that the direction of the wind altered in their favour when each man about to put out to sea stood astride the waters of this well for a few seconds.

The Lost Well of Youth is believed to have been on the slopes on Conachair. An aged St. Kildan is said to have discovered this well while carrying a sheep to the fold. Immediately he drank of its water, his decrepitude left him, and his youth returned. Surprised at finding water where formerly none ever had been seen, he laid down the sheep to mark the spot, and then hastened off to the village to inform the inhabitants. The villagers set out with him in great excitement. On arriving at the spot where he had left the sheep, they found no sign either of the well or of the sheep. And ever since that day the St. Kildans from time to time have referred to what they then named the Lost Well of Youth.

And they say that, had he placed a fragment of iron by the well, ere he left the sheep by it - a nail or tacket, or even an old fishing-hook - the Little Folks would not have been able to reclaim the well that had the power of restoring youth and vigour. It is held that the water of yet another well on St. Kilda 'will wash linen without soap as well as other water will with it.'

The well called Fivepennies

The most celebrated well in Jura was noted for the fact that its water was lighter by one-half than any other water in the island, with the result that one could consume large quantities of it without feeling the least uncomfortable. It was, moreover, a certain preventive against sea-sickness to whomsoever drank of it.

There are two wells in Eigg, which were reputed to be efficacious against ailments. Martin speaks of one called Fivepennies, which, he says, never failed to cure the natives. If a stranger should lie at this well during the night, he woke up with some deformity in the morning. But the inhabitants were immune to such deformities, even if they should have lain there for several nights. The other well on Eigg is called St. Catherine's Well. It is situated at the opposite end of the island, and was believed to be a catholicon for all diseases.

A well near to the village of Borve, in Harris, was long held to be efficacious in cases of loss of appetite. Even if one had eaten but an hour previously, a sip of water from this well readily restored the appetite alike of the native and the stranger.

The wells of Lewis

Near the Butt of Lewis is a well, the water of which was considered a remedy for insanity. Patients going there to be cured were first of all required to walk seven times round the Temple of St. Molochus, the ruins of which stand a few yards away.

It was called *Teampull Mór* in Gaelic, meaning the Great Temple. But this name must have referred only to its holiness, because the place was very small. Having journeyed round seven times, he who sought relief from madness was besprinkled with water, which was conveyed in a little jar from St. Ronan's Well. This jar was entrusted to the hereditary custody of a family whose early ancestors were designated 'the dark of the temple.' After the patient had been sprinkled with water, he was laid on the site of the altar, where, if he slept soundly, he was bound to recover from his malady.

St. Andrew's Well, in Lewis, was also consulted in cases of illness. From it a tub of water was borne to the bed-side of a sick person. Then a plate or a saucer was placed gently on the surface of the water. If this moved round sun-wise, the invalid was sure to recover: and, conversely, if it sank or moved round the other way, nothing but death could be expected.

In a churchyard close to the shore of Loch Torridon there is a well wherein for hundreds of years 'three stones have been perpetually shirled round and round.' By conveying one of these stones in a pail of water to a person afflicted with any kind of illness, a cure was effected whenever the patient placed his hand in the pail and touched the stone. But, alas! one fine day an old woman tried to cure her goat in this way; and, when she replaced the stone in the well, it no longer whirled, but sank to the bottom. Its virtue had vanished; and it has remained motionless ever since.

The wells of Barra

Near Loch St. Clair is a well which the natives of Barra call *Tobar Chaluim Chille*, **believing it to be the spring frequented by St. Columba.**

'And they were saying that St. Columba left a kind of spell on that well,' a native of Barra informed me some years ago. Generations of East Coast fishermen have been in the habit of calling this well St. Clair's Well. In olden times the fishermen of Barra used to drink of its water on Sundays, in the hope of getting heavy shots of herring during the week; and in pre-Reformation days, when the Church of St. Barr, at Eoligarry, was the only place of public worship in the Isle of Barra, the Islesfolk, sailing over from Vatersay and the other Barra Isles, used to slake their thirst at this well on the way to divine service.

Some there are who say that, before proceeding to church, the women-folk of these Islands were accustomed to tidy their hair when gazing at their reflections in the clear water of St. Clair's Well. We may take it that at this time mirrors were not included among the toilet requisites in vogue throughout the Barra Isles.

According to an ancient chronicler, 'there is one spring and fresh water Well. And the inhabitants and ancient men and women both men and women in this toune (Kilbar, in the north of Barra) and of the Countrie especiallie one ancient man being of fyve or sexscoir zeares old doth say that when appearance of Warrs wer to be in the Countrey of Barray that certaine drops of blood hath oftymes bein sein in this spring and fresh water Well.'

The chronicler emphasises the fact that, in addition to the testimony of the older inhabitants, he had this information corroborated by Rory MacNeil, the Chief of Barra at that time. Rory went a step further in alleging that, indicative of the coming of peace, 'certaine little bitts of Peitts wold be sein' in the well. But, then, we must take into account that at this time Rory MacNeil was 'ane veric ancient man of sexscoir yeares old or therby,' and that the most insistent informant was 'fyve or sexscoir zeares.'

The most famous well in Barra, of course, is that associated with the cockles of the Great Cockle Shore, in the north of the island. This is the well referred to by Martin as the Well of Kilbar, which, he writes, 'throws up embryoes of cockles, but I could not discern any in the rivulet, the air being at the time foggy.'

A son's revenge

In that part of the Isle of Skye known as Strath there is a well known as *Tobar a' Chinn*, Well of the Head. It was here that a certain Lauchlan MacKinnon avenged himself on Donnachadh Mór by beheading him and washing his head in this well.

Donnachadh Mór was ground-officer to MacKinnon of Strath. In the course of his rounds he exacted from a poor widow the oppressive death-duty called the *each-ursainn*. In tribal days it was the custom in the Highlands for the laird's factor to remove from the relatives of a deceased tenant their best horse or cow. On this occasion the widow resisted Donnachadh's claim; but he ill-used her, and took the horse from her by force.

Now, Lauchlan MacKinnon had learnt as a youngster from his own mother that, when she became a widow, she had suffered similar treatment at the hands of the same factor. For years, therefore, he waited for an opportunity of paying off this old score against Donnachadh; and here, he decided, was the opportunity. He engaged the factor, killed him, decapitated him, and washed his head in the Well of the Head. And it is said in Skye that thereafter no factor dared exact the ancient death-duty known as the *each-ursainn*.

This recalls the story connected with the famous well by the roadside at Loch Oich, and known as the Well of the Seven Heads. But this story is more a matter of history than of folk tale. Over this well there stands a tall monument; and carved in stone on the four sides is a long inscription in English, Gaelic, French and Latin.

In this wise runs the English inscription: 'As a memorial of the example and summary vengeance which, in the swift course of feudal justice, inflicted by the order of Lord McDonell and Aross, overtook the perpetrators of the foul murder of the Keppoch Family, a branch of the powerful and illustrious clan of which his lordship was the chief. This monument is erected by Colonel McDonell of Glengarry, XVII Mac-Mhic-Alaister, his successor and representative, in the year of Our Lord 1812. The heads of the Seven Murderers were presented at the feet of the noble Chief in Glengarry Castle after having been washed in this spring; and ever since that event, which took place in the sixteenth century, it has been known by the name of *Tobar-nan-Ceann* or the Well of the Heads.'

The springs that made a loch

From mythological times there has been handed down to us the folk tale of how Loch Awe came into existence. According to this tale, that dreaded female demon, the Cailleach Bheur, whose exploits are recorded in the folklore of several countries, had occasion to pass through the valley now occupied by Loch Awe, when, as if by evil design, her foot struck an obstacle. Thus released, it is believed, were the subterranean springs that now welled up to fill the valley with a loch.

According to the Ossianic version of this folk tale, a wise man, who lay dying, sent for his fair daughter, Bera, and bequeathed to her as the last of her race all the fertile farmlands now submerged beneath the waters of Loch Awe. Only one condition did he attach to the bequest - namely, that every evening at sundown Bera should ascend to a spring on the summit of Ben Cruachan, and on the mouth of that spring place a sacred stone, so as to prevent its waters from flowing down to cover the face of the valley.

Bera regularly fulfilled her father's instructions after his death. But one day, weary with hunting the corries of Cruachan, she fell asleep on the sunny hillside. Not until the third morning did she awaken; and by that time her heritage lay beneath the waters of the loch that since then has been known as Loch Awe.

The great escape

There is a cave at Urkaig Beag, in Colonsay, of which the following story is told. The last of the MacPhee lairds of Colonsay had been defeated by his enemies, the MacNeils, and took refuge along with his three dogs in this cave, which had an entrance from the sea, and another from the land.

At the sea entrance MacPhee placed his three dogs on guard against his enemies, while he himself took up a defensive position in a recess about halfway down the cave, where there was just room enough to enable him to wield his sword. At this point the main cave is so contracted that it is necessary for one to get on all-fours in order to pass through. As MacPhee saw the head of each of his pursuers emerge in turn from the contracted passage, he promptly beheaded him, and dragged his corpse into the cave.

When this fate had befallen five or six of his foes, the remainder, unable to obtain any response to their enquiry as to how fared their accomplices, took alarm. After consultation, they agreed to dig down into the cave from above. This, MacPhee realised, would mean his disaster. Meanwhile recognising the tide to have risen sufficiently at the sea entrance to prevent his enemies from gaining ingress except by swimming, he decided, while their attention was diverted in digging above, to escape by swimming across Kiloran Bay, along with his dogs, a distance of about a mile.

He had not completed a bow-shot's length of this arduous undertaking, however, when his foes noticed him, and discharged a flight of arrows at him, one of which pierced his hip. MacPhee now made for a rock lying a little ahead, landed thereon, and extracted the arrow. Since that day the rock has been known by a Gaelic name meaning the Black Skerry of MacPhee.

Thereafter MacPhee and his dogs completed their swim across Kiloran Bay. They then wandered along the shore until they came to Baile na h-Airde. There MacPhee found a coble with a plank stove in, lying amongst iris-flags above high-water mark. Cutting a sward with his knife, he plugged the leak, and launched the coble. And, taking his dogs aboard with him, he rowed across to Jura. In this wise he escaped from the cave on Colonsay that to this day is known as MacPhee's Cave.

Suffocated to death

There is a folk-tale current in Ardnamurchan that recalls the manner in which the MacLeods of Sky suffocated the MacDonalds, who had taken refuge in the Cave of St. Frances, on the Island of Eigg.

Tradition has it that the whereabouts of the MacDonalds were disclosed by the footprints of one of their number who, believing the enemy to be out of sight, came out of the cave to reconnoitre, and left his marks upon the snow, thus enabling the enemy to trace him and his clansmen to their hiding-place.

By the rocky shore of Ardnamurchan there is a cave known as the cave of the MacIans. At the time of the story, Ardnamurchan belonged to a sept of the MacDonalds called the MacIans of Ardnamurchan. Now, about the year 1624, the Campbells invaded Ardnamurchan, seized the MacIan stronghold of Mingary, garrisoned it, and drove the MacIans into hiding among the wilds of their patrimony.

Some of the fugitives sought refuge in this cave. Here they might have remained undetected for a time, had not one of them, weary of his confinement in the dark cavern, come out into the open, and left his footprints in the previous night's fall of snow. It is said that the fugitive on realising the jeopardy into which he carelessly had thrown himself and his clans-people, endeavoured to cover up his tracks by retreating backwards toward the cave; but how it was imagined this would deceive anyone, no one can explain.

In any case, one of the Clan Campbell had observed him, and had hurried off to Mingary Castle, which was now in the possession of his kinsmen. Forthwith a detachment of Campbells reconnoitred the footprints, and traced them to the cave, wherein were huddled several of the MacIans. At the mouth of the cave they kindled a great fire, and thus suffocated its occupants to death.

If this incident be true, as well it may be, it occurred just half a century after the somewhat similar incident on the Island of Eigg, when the MacLeods entrapped the MacDonalds in the Cave of St. Frances, and at the entrance to that cave maintained a fire 'with unrelenting assiduity,' to use Sir Walter Scott's words.

An evil deed

Upon a time there stood on the moor between Dunvegan and Stein, in the Vaternish district of Skye, a haunted house, with which is associated the following witch tale.

In this house there dwelt a woman and her son. One day, while the woman was out at the peats and her son was snoozing on the wooden settle that to this day forms so indispensable a part of the furniture of an island home, three black cats entered by the window, and immediately took the shape of women. Their visit was with evil intent: they had made their way into the house as cats, so as to conceal their identity.

There now followed a prolonged discussion; and it was only when their deliberations were drawing to a close that the witches realised the son had been feigning sleep all the time, and had overheard their malevolent scheme. Thereupon one of them addressed him sternly, and warned him not to repeat a word they had uttered, adding that, if he did so, he would suffer for it. Having intimidated the boy into promising that he would not give them away, the three witches again assumed the form of cats, and left the house as they had entered.

Now, the boy, when he thought that all likelihood of the witches carrying out their threat was passed, told their secret to his mother, who in turn vowed that she would never mention the matter to a soul. However, some time afterwards a violent dispute ensued between the mother and one of the witches, in the course of which the former completely lost her head, and said something that convinced the witch that the boy had broken his word.

That night the three witches met, and arranged to waylay the boy in the dark. Their ambush was successful, and there was found between the Faery Bridge and Stein the lifeless body of the unhappy lad. 'And, if you're not believing me,' emphasised the raconteur who gave me this tale, 'there's a sign on the roadside between the Faery Bridge and Stein to prove it!'

Soon afterwards the folks of the neighbourhood raised a cairn to mark the spot where the foul deed had been committed; but today the *Carn a'Ghille*, or Lad's Cairn, is not to be seen. The belief is that it may have sunk down into the peaty soil, and gradually disappeared from view. But the spot is said to be haunted; and even yet children, who have been told the story of the three witches, hesitate to pass this way after nightfall. In fact, I have met elderly people in Skye who deliberately avoid this crossing-place in the dark, when possible.

The drowning of Iain Garbh

It was through the schemings of witches that one of the MacLeods of Raasay lost his life. This MacLeod was greatly disliked by the Skye witches, because he was wont to deal out rough justice to them when they defaulted in any way. Eventually they arranged to assemble by the shore at the Narrows of Raasay, not far from the Braes, and to watch for his galley when it was likely to be sailing between his island home and Portree.

This they did; and on one occasion, when they perceived his boat to be a convenient distance from the shore, a picked contingent of them was transformed into cats, and made for the boat. By huddling together at the poop, they capsized it. Thus MacLeod was drowned. Thereafter the cats swam ashore in great exultation, and once more resumed their human appearance.

Witchcraft is also believed to have encompassed the death of that dauntless member of the family of MacLeod of Raasay called Iain Garbh. An entry in the year 1671, in the *Polichronon*, that most illuminating record of the Highlands written during the seventeenth century by James Fraser, minister of Wardlaw, throws the following contemporary light on the untimely death of Iain Clarbh MacLeod of Raasay:

'This April the Earle of Seaforth duelling in the Lewes, a dreedful accident happened. His lady being brought to bed there, the Earle sent for John Garve M'kleud of Rarsay, to witness the christning; and, after the treat and solmnity of the feast, Rarsay takes leave to goe home, and, after a rant of drinking upon the shoare, went aboord off his birling and sailed away with a strong north gale off wind; and whither by giving too much saile and no ballast, or the unskillfulness of the seamen, or that they could not mannage the strong Dut(ch) canvas saile, the boat whelmd, and all the men around in view of the cost. The Laird and sixteen of his kinsmen, the prime, perished; non of them ever found; a grewhound or two cast ashoare dead; and pieces of the birling. One Alexander Mackleod of Lewes the night before had voice warning him thrice not to goe at (all) with Rarsay, for all would drown in their return; yet he went with him, being infatuat, and dround (with) the rest. This account I had from Alexander his brother the summer after. Drunkness did the (mischeife).'

The story is told in the Isles that a raven flew ominously round Iain's boat while he was returning across the Minch from Stornoway. The raven eventually settled on the gunwale; and Iain Garbh drew his dirk in an attempt to kill it. But he missed the mark; and so colossal was his strength that the point of the dirk clove the timbers instead, with the result that the boat rapidly sank with all hands.

The raven, they say, was a witch in disguise, who had been hired by Iain's stepmother. She was inimical toward him, as stepmothers often are toward stepchildren who have inherited what they coveted for their own children.

But Donald Gorm of Sleat is said to have had a hand in the drowning of Iain Garbh MacLeod of Raasay to the extent that he promised the witch a profitable stretch of land in Trotternish, if she carried out his directions.

In the folklore of Skye, the witch's name is given as Morag. When Donald Gorm made his offer to her, she retired to the seclusion of her peat-fire, and sat over it for several hours in deep meditation. Then she summoned her daughter, and directed her to bring a large tub from the byre, and to fetch water from the well. The tub was duly filled to the brim. Thereafter Morag set an eggshell afloat in the tub. Then she betook herself to a high hill in the neighbourhood, overlooking the sea, where for three days and three nights she watched for the coming of Iain Garbh's birlinn. About noon on the fourth day, she recognised the birlinn approaching under a favourable wind. When it came fairly close inshore, she rushed home and instructed her daughter to stir the water in the tub.

Soon it was noticed by those assembled by the shore, awaiting Iain Garbh's arrival, that the birlinn was in serious straits. A squall enveloped her; and she sank with all hands. And the natives of Skye used to say that, on the anniversary of Iain Garbh's drowning, the incoming tide always made a great commotion just at the spot where he and his men fell victim to witchcraft.

But some time afterwards the witch and Donald Gorm fell out. Not long after the drowning of Iain Garbh, she herself was found drowned by the shore of Raasay; and the folks of Skye and of the adjacent Isles had a shrewd suspicion that Donald Gorm was responsible.

A witch caught red-footed

There once lived in the Sleat of Skye a dairymaid who was continually pestered by a cat that, for its size, had an abnormal capacity for milk. For years this creature had been helping itself to milk; and every precaution to exclude it from the dairy proved futile. Futile, too, were all attempts to capture it.

At last the long-suffering dairymaid was able to get her revenge, for one day the cat, having consumed so much milk that it scarcely could crawl, was caught red-footed! With a chopper that lay to hand, the dairymaid chopped off one of its ears.

Not long afterwards she was aghast at finding that a woman living but a few doors away had lost an ear. And so ashamed of herself was the victim that she never ventured across her own threshold except when her head was completely covered by a plaid or shawl.

Turned into a horse

Loch Bracadale also has its witch story. Angus, the favourite man-servant of the tacksman of Ullinish, had an extraordinary experience. At all times he and his employer were the best of friends; but, albeit they had the utmost confidence in one another, Angus was loth to tell his master why he always looked so tired before the day's work began.

In course of time the state of Angus's health gave the tacksman so much concern that he approached him in a fatherly way, and persuaded him to reveal the cause of his condition. And it transpired that poor Angus was the dupe of a woman whom he declared to have been a witch. When at night he came in from his work and was eager to lie down and rest, she used to throw a halter round his neck and transform him into a horse, on whose back she galloped all over Skye to attend witch meetings during the night-time. They never returned until morning, with the result that Angus was usually too tired to be able for his daily routine about the farm.

Angus's story greatly perturbed the tacksman of Ullinish; and so, without breathing a word to anyone, he and Angus decided that the next time the witch came on the scene, Angus would take the bridle forcibly from her, and reiterate to her the phrases she had been in the habit of repeating when transforming him into a horse. Furthermore, the tacksman instructed Angus to shoe her with real horse-shoes immediately she was changed, and to restore her to her normal condition after he had had a jaunt with her round the countryside.

That very night, to be sure, the witch again was at her black art. Angus did not fail to carry out the instructions he and the tacksman of Ullinish had agreed upon. Next morning, when the family was assembling for breakfast, the tacksman kept on wondering and wondering why his wife was so long in making her appearance. When at length he went to look for her, he found her ill in bed. So he straightway sent for a physician, who on arrival discovered a pair of horse-shoes so firmly nailed to her feet that they could not be removed.

And before long the tacksman was lamenting the loss of his wife who, to his amazement, had been practised in the Black Art.

Loch of the sword

Perhaps one of the best known witch tales in Scotland is that associated with a small loch lying a mile or so to the north of Rannoch Station, in the very heart of Scotland, exactly where the boundaries of the three great counties of Inverness, Argyll, and Perth meet. The loch, which is of no great dimensions, goes by a Gaelic name meaning the Loch of the Sword; and as such it is shown on the map.

It is related that, about three centuries ago, there arose between representatives of the family of Atholl and Locheil, Chief of the Clan Cameron, a dispute as to the ownership of some lands in the neighbourhood. Wellnigh every means of settlement had been exhausted; and the two clans, weary of continual warfare, eagerly sought to compose their difference by mutual agreement. So, after a considerable amount of fruitless strife, Atholl and the worthy Chief of the Camerons arranged that they would meet one another alone on a certain day by the loch aforementioned, and there endeavour to arrive at a peaceful solution in regard to the lands in dispute.

When the appointed day arrived, and Locheil was on his way to the place where he had promised to meet Atholl, he was accosted on the moor by a frail and aged woman, who asked him: 'Where are your men, Locheil? Where are your men, Locheil?'

To her question the Chief paid little attention, and turned quietly toward her and said: 'Hold thy peace, old witch! I have no need for my gallant men today, for I travel to a loch where Atholl has agreed to meet me alone.'

So Locheil continued on his way. But the old woman limped after him, and, having seized hold of his tartan plaid, persisted in interrogating him again, for she felt that, if the Chief of the Camerons intended proceeding unaccompanied to the loch, he might find himself in danger. 'Where are your men, Locheil? Where are your men?' she kept on repeating.

Locheil now began to feel a little perturbed by her insistence; and he realised that, if anything unforeseen were to occur when he came face to face with Atholl, he would never forgive himself for ignoring the warning. And, therefore, he hurried off to the nearest clachan and collected a band of men, that he might be prepared in the event of any emergency. This bodyguard he directed to follow after him, and to conceal itself among the bracken and heather by the side of the loch, lest he should require its assistance.

In course of time the two chiefs met face to face; but their efforts to come to terms produced naught but wrath and acrimony. Atholl was determined not to yield an inch of the territory in dispute; and any suggestion that he should merely exasperated him. When he found that he could endure things no longer, he waved his hand, whereupon there leapt up from the heather, in which they had concealed themselves beforehand, twenty stalwart Atholl Highlanders.

'Who are these?' angrily enquired Locheil.

'Oh!' replied Atholl with a smile of disdain, 'these are Atholl wethers who have come to graze on Locheil's pastures.'

Now Locheil had arranged with his men that, whenever he required their help, he would expose the inside of his cloak. This he now did; and instantly three score of his warriors came dashing down the hillside to the scene of the rivalry, and eagerly awaited instructions from their chief.

'Who are these, Locheil?' asked Atholl, now speechless with surprise.

'Ah, these are Locheil's dogs,' responded the Chief of the Clan Cameron. 'They are sharp of tooth and famishing; and, what's more, they are indeed keen to sample the flesh of your Atholl wethers. You must renounce your claim to these lands instantly, for I cannot hold these fierce creatures by the chain much longer!'

As the result of this alarming episode the chiefs, without further delay, came to terms in favour of Locheil. And Atholl, having drawn his sword from its sheath, kissed it, swung it over his head, and pitched it into the loch, declaring in so doing that the lands in dispute would belong to Locheil until such time as the sword might be recovered.

While fishing in *Lochan a' Chlaidheimh*, the Lochan of the Sword, about the beginning of the nineteenth century, a schoolboy accidentally dragged the basket-hilted claymore up again, and handed it over to the parish minister. But the men of Locheil were so alarmed, on learning that the sword had been found, that they pleaded with the minister to deliver it up to them, so that they might deposit it in the loch once more. To their wish the minister conceded; and, so, to this very day Atholl's sword lies in this loch, which is little more than a moorland tarn.

Such is the story of the Loch of the Sword, where Atholl discreetly surrendered his claim to the lands - 'through summer's heat and winter's cold.'

Phantom light

When an Edinburgh doctor, who some years ago was staying at an inn at Broadford, went out after supper one evening for a turn along the beach, he noticed far out in the bay a very bright light, which he took to be a flare ignited by fishermen. But the light came smoothly and steadily toward the spot where he was standing. The doctor described it as being like a globe of light, such as one might find on a lampstandard in an up-to-date city.

Whenever the light touched the shore, it disappeared; and a cloaked woman, bearing a child in her arms, now hurried across the sand in front of him, and vanished in a moment.

The doctor now returned to his quarters, and questioned the innkeeper as to whether he was aware of any strange occurrence that might have accounted for this unearthly experience. With some reluctance the innkeeper told him that, several years earlier, there had been a shipwreck in the bay, and that a woman and child had been cast ashore, dead, on the beach, just at the spot he described.

This weird apparition - if such it may be called - has not been seen often. But the innkeeper stated that occasionally it is observed by the natives of the district about the time of year when the shipwreck aforesaid occurred.

Haunted lochs

A phenomenon of a similar character is associated with Loch Rannoch, where a light in the form of a ball sometimes is seen skimming the surface of the water. This light always rises at the same point, travels the same short distance, and likewise disappears at the same place. On occasions, however, it has been observed to rise from the water, and roll up the hill called Meall-dubh. Only a few years ago the natives of Loch Rannoch-side witnessed this strange loch light.

It may be mentioned here that Loch Ness has its apparition, as well as its monster. It is known to the Highlanders as the Old Man of Inverfarigaig. 'The Bodach,' as he is called locally, often is seen in the woods among the rocks at Inverfarigaig. But he is oftener heard than seen. In time of winter storm, he can be heard shrieking among the leafless trees fringing Loch Ness at Inverfarigaig.

Two bright balls of fire

There is a story told in Breadalbain of two *gealbhain*, or balls of fire, which were seen flitting over the face of Loch Tay.

A small farm at Morenish, on Loch Tay-side, was tenanted by a family of the name of Cameron; and, while the eldest son was serving abroad with the army, his two brothers died of fever, and were buried in the churchyard at Kenmore. When the surviving brother came home on furlough, he decided to exhume the coffins containing their remains, and to carry them by water to the other end of Loch Tay, for re-interment at Killin.

On the night preceding the day of re-interment, two bright balls of fire were witnessed rolling along the surface of the loch in the very course afterwards followed by the boat conveying the coffins. It is not so very long since there lived in Glen Lochay one of the many natives of this district, who witnessed this weird spectacle.

This recalls another strange fragment, still recounted in Breadalbain, concerning a ferryman who lived on the north side of Loch Tay, and who one evening heard a shrill whistle as of someone wanting to cross the loch from the opposite shore. He immediately made for his boat, and rowed over toward the usual ferrying-place on the south side.

However, on his arriving there, not a soul did he find. But, as he rested for a moment, an ungainly object, resembling a large sack of wool, came rolling down the brae, and toppled into his boat. Too terrified to examine the nature of his cargo, he proceeded to row home again. Immediately the boat touched the north shore, the ungainly cargo assumed the form of a huge, white bird, which, with a great screeching and flapping of wings, soared away to the burying-place of Lawers.

Only a day or two after this, the ferryman found himself conveying across Loch Tay from the south side the corpse of a young woman who died suddenly, and who was interred duly in the old burying-place of Lawers.

Two Breadalbain spirits

There is told among the clachans fringing the shores of Loch Tay, and indeed throughout Breadalbain, the story of a ghost that haunted the farmhouse of Claggan, on the south side of the loch. On one occasion at least, this ghost, when on its nocturnal errands, assumed the form of a dog. So disturbed became the countryside as the result of ghost rumours, that the inhabitants eventually refused to pass anywhere near Claggan after dusk.

One evening an elderly man crossed Loch Tay from the Lawers side, with the intention of paying a visit to his sister, who was married to a tenant-farmer at Ardtalnaig. No sooner had he reached within shouting distance of the farmhouse of Claggan than a huge, grey dog appeared by a heap of stones known locally as *An Cam Mor*, the Big Cairn. The old man did his best to continue his journey without showing any fear; and he observed that the dog moved forward with him in a parallel line, some yards away, that it stopped when he stopped, started again when he started, and hastened when he hastened, for all the world like an ominous shadow.

At length the old man reached Claggan farmhouse, where, in passing by the front, he received some temporary relief on finding that his escort had disappeared. But no sooner had he reached the farther gable than he again was confronted with this eerie creature. Terror-stricken, he turned back, and dashed into the farmhouse, where he fainted in the arms of its occupants.

When he came to, the MacKays, who were tenants of Claggan Farm, addressed him: 'What was it frightened you, John? Were you seeing anything?'

John then proceeded to tell them of his experience with the strange dog. By this time he was so unnerved that he asked three or four of the younger men about the farm to escort him the remaining mile of his journey to Ardtalnaig, where his sister lived. But MacKay himself had been so moved by the supernatural nature of John's story that he would not hear of anyone quitting his hearth that night.

Also connected with Breadalbain is the folk tale of a ghost that attempted to lie its full length in an open coffin, in order to demonstrate to those concerned that the coffin was too short for the corpse for which it was intended.

There had died at one of the townships overlooking Loch Tay a man, whose body the local joiner had measured for kisting. On the evening of the day on which the coffin was completed, a footsore and weary beggar came to the joiner's door, seeking a night's shelter. The joiner's wife informed him that, although there was no room available in the house, she had no objection to his spending the night in her husband's workshop, so long as he did not mind the empty coffin lying on the bench. The wood-shavings, she observed, would make a soft, clean bed for him.

The beggar was too weary that night to have any qualms about accepting such an offer on account of an empty coffin; and scarcely a moment was he on his bed of shavings when he noticed a spectre, shrouded in white, climb up on the bench, and attempt to stretch itself out in the coffin that, obviously, was too short for it. The spectre then vanished; and the beggar decided to make the best of his shelter until morning.

'That coffin is too short for the body you want to put in it!' said the beggar to the joiner on the following morning.

'Why that?' enquired the joiner.

'Well, last night,' continued the beggar, 'I saw the ghost called of the dead man trying to get into it, and he couldn't.'

The joiner laughed at the vagrant, to whom he and his wife had given a night's roofing; but, as a matter of interest, he though he would just measure the corpse again, and compare its length with that of the empty coffin. And, sure enough, as the beggar had indicated, the coffin had to be enlarged.

Ocean of the Spectre

Long before the MacNeil Chiefs evacuated Kisimul Castle to take up residence at Eoligarry, in the northern peninsula of the Island of Barra, the following folk tale was prevalent in Mingulay, and indeed throughout the Barra Isles.

In the days before local girls were employed so extensively during the fishing seasons at Castlebay and similar herring-curing ports, it was customary for Barra girls to seek domestic employment in Ireland. In those days there was a continual coming and going between Barra and Ireland. Irish cargo boats, carrying seed potatoes and the like, frequently called at Castlebay; and the captains of these vessels usually were willing to convey over to Erin such islanders as were eager to go into service in that country.

Now, a girl from the Isle of Pabbay and another from Mingulay had planned secretly that they would avail themselves of the first opportunity to going over to Erin. One day, while the Mingulay girl was lifting a creel of peats on her back, she beheld a strange man standing in front of her. How he had come to remote Mingulay without her knowing it was a mystery to her. She passed the time of day with him; and in the course of a brief conversation he referred to the voyage to Erin contemplated by herself and her Pabbay companion. He foretold that, while she would settle contentedly in her new surroundings, her Pabbay friend would die in Ireland of fever.

While speaking to the stranger, the Mingulay girl chanced to observe a sailing-vessel some miles off the coast. In a trice this vessel capsized; and all its occupants were precipitated into the sea. Screaming with shock, she strove to draw the stranger's attention to the scene of the fatality. But he assured her that the incident she had just witnessed had no application whatsoever to people then living - the grand-parents of those thrown into the sea, he explained, were not yet born.

When the girl returned home with her creel of peats, she told her people of the interview with a man unknown to her, and of the weird apparition she had beheld. And on the locality, in which she declared the incident to have occurred, her people put the name of *Cuan a'Bhochdain*, Ocean of the Spectre.

About forty years ago a small fishing-vessel capsized in this neighbourhood, and all hands perished.

And now to the sequel.

While stationed in Northern Ireland, a soldier belonging to Barra, and in his day widely known in these parts as the Pearsanach Mór, deserted the army. In the course of his flight, he came to a cottage that was being re-thatched. Upon entering, he told the housewife that he was a native of the Isle of Barra; and he confessed to his being a military deserter. He pleaded with her to conceal him, since the military police were hot in pursuit of him. The goodwife hastened out to her husband, who at the time was busy with the thatching of his cottage. As the result of a brief conversation with him, it was decided that the Pearsanach Mór would be concealed under the thatch until the scare was past.

Barely a minute was the deserter under the thatch when armed men rode up to the cottage, and enquired of the thatcher whether he had noticed a fugitive pass by. To this interrogation they received a reply in the negative. So they sped on in the direction in which they imagined the deserter to have gone. On reaching the point beyond which they knew no human being could have fled in so short a time, they returned to the cottage and insisted on searching it. House, byre, stable, loft were ransacked; but no deserter did they find. Whereupon they gave up the pursuit, and returned to their quarters.

Toward the evening of the same day, the husband opened up the thatch and extricated the Pearsanach Mór. Now the goodwife did a certain amount of weaving in her spare moments; and her brother-in-law was a tai-lor. So, between them, they made a new suit to take the place of the fugitive's uniform, which he already had discarded. And it was while the Pearsanach Mór sojourned at this cottage in Northern Ireland that he learnt of his hostess that it was she who, as a girl, had seen in the Ocean of the Spectre the extraordinary apparition, of which he had heard tell in his boyhood days. She declared to him that the foretellings of the stranger, who confronted her when creeling peats on Mingulay, had come true - she was settled happily in Ireland, and her Pabbay companion had died of fever years before.

As I have just mentioned, it is only about forty years since the final part of this prophecy was witnessed in the loss in the *Cuan a' Bhochdain*, in the Ocean of the Spectre, of a fishing-boat with all hands.

The folks of the Barra Isles still affirm that the occupants of this boat were the great-grand-children of a family once living on Mingulay, whose unborn posterity was associated with the accident at the time of its spectral happening.

Truly, this is a ghost tale, and a tale of the 'second sight.'

Washer of the death-shrouds

One of the strangest of all apparitions is the *bean-nighe*, or washing-woman. For one to see the washing of the death-shrouds by the *bean-nighe* in some lonely and remote loch, or in the eerie pool of a river, and sometimes even at a fording-place, was regarded as one of the commonest warnings of death in the Highlands and Hebrides. The *bean-nighe* might be observed by a ford, diligently washing the linen of persons about to be overtaken by death, or folding and beating the linen as it lay on a stone almost entirely submerged in the water.

In Perthshire the washing-woman is described as a creature, small and rotund, and clad in flimsy raiment of emerald hue. The person seeing her, it was held, must not hurry away, but should try to steal up behind her, and surprise her by asking for whom she was washing the death-shrouds.

In Skye, however, she has been likened to a squat creature resembling a small, pitiful child. If caught when 'dreeing her weird,' she related to her captor what fate awaited him. She responded to all his questionings, if assured that her captor would answer truthfully all questions she, in turn, put to him.

If the person approaching a washing-woman were able to get his hands on her before she either saw or heard him, and she meanwhile engaged with the shrouds, he was able to detain her, and demand of her an answer to his interrogations. If, on the other hand, he was observed or heard by her in his approach, she was able to deprive him of the use of his limbs.

There is a tradition in the Alvie district of Inverness-shire that one of the lochans set in the surrounding hills was the haunt of such a washing-woman. Visible only to those under the shadow of death was this phantom washer of the shrouds. It was held that she represented the disembodied spirit of a mother, who had died in childbirth, and whose garments had not all been washed at the time of her burial. Since death at childbirth was regarded as premature and unpropitious, the phantom washing-woman of Alvie continued to rinse in this lochan the shirts of all those who were fated to die or be killed in battle between the date of the mother's death and the date on which she would have died in the natural course of events.

One of the most popular of Highland stories connected with the washing of the death-shrouds is told of the Mermaid of Loch Slin. On turning a corner on the path by the side of this loch one Sabbath morning, a Cromarty maiden was startled at finding what seemed to be a tall female who, standing in the water just beyond a cluster of flags and rushes, was 'knocking claes' on a stone with a bludgeon. On a bleaching-green near at hand she observed more than thirty smocks and shirts, all horribly besmeared with blood. Shortly after the appearance of this apparition, the roof of Fearn Abbey collapsed during worship, burying the congregation in its debris, and killing thirty-six. This accounted for the strange washing by the banks of Loch Slin.

Missing fingers

Among the many places in Western Argyll that are said to be haunted is the strip of land separating the old burying-ground of Keil, in Morven, from the waters of the Sound of Mull. Both in Mull and in Morven tradition has it that, when the warlike MacLeans sent to the bottom of Tobermory Bay that wandered galleon of the Armada known as the *Florida*, there was a Spanish princess aboard. The princess was one of the many who perished.

Now, it is said that her body was recovered later, and that it was interred at Keil. A year or two ago, I had it from some of the natives of Morven, with whom I have a certain filial association, that, some time after the destruction of King Philip's proud fleet, there came to Morven a Spanish vessel, in order to bear the princess's remains to her native land. During the exhuming of her body, however, some of her finger bones were lost; and at times the ghost of the princess may be seen, as it flits between Keil and the shore of the Sound of Mull, seeking the lost finger bones.

And I actually have met folks in Morven who have encountered this ghost, and who avoid that piece of territory lying between Keil and the Sound of Mull, except in the broadest of daylight.

A warning of death

**The story is told in the Isle of Benbecula of the way in which a hench-
man of *Mac 'ic Ailein nan Eilean* - the Captain of Clan Ranald of the
Isles - was forewarned of the death of his valiant and beloved chieftain.
This henchman was known as the *Gille-cas-fluich*, the Lad of the Wet
Foot, simply because it was his duty to be walking constantly in front of
his master, so as to take the dew or the rain off grass and heather that
otherwise would be soaking his master's feet.**

Now, it was the Lad of the Wet Foot who, having come on the washing-woman, while she was wailing a death-dirge by one of the Benbecula
fords, seized hold of her, and refused to let her go until he learned of her for
whom she was washing the death-shroud and singing the dirge.

'Let me go,' said she, 'and give me the freedom of my feet, and that
the breeze of reek coming from thy grizzled tawny beard is anear putting a
stop to the breath of my throat. Much more would my nose prefer, and much
rather would my heart desire, the air of the fragrant incense of the mist of
the mountains.'

'I will not allow thee away,' replied the Lad of the Wet Foot, 'till
thou promise me my three choice desires!'

'Let me hear them, ill man!' said the *bean-nighe*.

'That thou wilt tell to me for whom thou art washing the shroud and
crooning the dirge, that thou wilt give me my choice spouse, and that thou
wilt keep abundant seaweed in the creek of our townland as long as the carle
of Sgeirrois shall continue his moaning.'

Then answered the *bean-nighe*: 'I am washing the shroud and
crooning the dirge for Great Clan Ranald of the Isles; and he shall never
again in his living life of the world go thither nor come hither across the
clachan of Dun Borve.'

Instantly the Lad of the Wet Foot grasped the death-shroud, and
flung it into the loch. And he hastened home to the stronghold of Dun Borve,
home to the bedside of Clan Ranald himself. And he related to his master all
that the washing-woman had told him at the stepping-stones by the ford, in
the dead of night.

Clan Ranald immediately directed that a cow be killed, and that
without delay a new coracle be made with the hide, so that he might be taking a long, long sail - no one knew whither. In no time the coracle was
brought to him. And Clan Ranald of the Isles speedily forsook Dun Borve,

carrying the coracle; and he could be seen in the act of paddling himself away and away, out over the loch. And never again, either on moorland or on machar, or by the shore of sea or loch, was the Captain of Clan Ranald seen in human form in Benbecula.

A woman's fear

Mention of death and the death-shrouds reminds one of the fact that, if there were one thing elderly or aged Highlanders and Islanders dreaded more than another, it was the idea that they might die among strangers, and at a distance from their homes. The extent to which this notion still prevails among them is shown by the exertions, both physical and financial, they often make to bring home, sometimes from very far away, the corpse of a relative, so that it may rest finally with the dust of their forbears. Few happenings were regarded as more calamitous than that one should be consigned to the earth among strangers, and away from the care and sympathy of relatives.

An incident illustrative of this is mentioned by General Stewart of Garth in his *Sketches*. A Highland woman, aged ninety-one, and possessed of all her faculties, had left her home in Strathbraan to visit a daughter residing in Perth. A few days after her arrival at Perth, she developed a mild fever. A heavy fall of snow at this time quite discomposed her; and, when she was told that a heavier fall was expected, her anxiety increased so considerably that she decided to slip away during the night, and make for her home in Strathbraan, some twenty miles off. In the morning the daughter discovered an empty bed.

Not until a couple of days afterwards did she learn what had happened. Her mother sent word that she had set out at midnight to trudge home through the snow, and that she did not halt, even to draw breath, until she reached her own threshold. When interrogated later as to what had induced her to set out on so perilous an adventure at her time of life, she responded: 'If my sickness had increased, and I had died, they could not have sent my remains home through the deep snow. If I had told my daughter, maybe she would have locked the room on me, and God forbid that my bones should be at such a distance from home, and be buried among the *Gall na Machair*, among the Strangers of the Plain!'

The singular predilection Highlanders have for their own country, and especially for their place of birth, is shown in the following tale, still told in Perthshire, of an old man who once tenanted a farm at the base of Schiehallion. In his latter years he went to reside with a son, who had taken a farm a goodly distance farther down the country. One morning the old man went out, and was missing for a considerable time. When he returned eventually, he was asked to explain his prolonged absence. 'As I was seated by the river,' he replied, 'the thought came to me that, maybe, some of the waters from Schiehallion, and the sweet fountains that watered the farm of my forefathers, might be passing by me, and that, if I bathed, they might touch my skin. So I stripped; and from the pleasure of being immersed in the pure waters of Schiehallion could not tear myself away!'

Jacobite tales

It may be said without fear of serious contradiction that the Risings of 1715 and 1745, culminating as they did in the final overthrow of the Jacobites at Culloden, constitute the only outstanding phase of Scottish history since the arrival of Columba, or of Ninian.

The Scottish War of Independence with all its adventures of Wallace and Bruce, the Cromwellian activities north of the Tweed, the Union of the Crowns and, later, of the Parliaments, were all important in their way; but not one of them raised Scotland out of the drab, monotonous succession of minor battles and political intrigues and skirmishes. Bannockburn, it is true, has its peculiar significance for every Scot the world over; but the rout of Edward was of less consequence even to Scotland than Culloden - the last and greatest outburst of Highland chivalry.

It is not to be wondered at, therefore, that these attempts to regain a kingdom forfeited, as we know, by crass intolerance and imprudence, should have given rise to a wealth of folk tale and tradition of a most fascinating nature. So indelible an impression did 'the Forty-five' make upon the people of Scotland that to this day it is quite a usual occurrence to come in contact with natives of the Highlands and Islands who speak of Prince Charlie as though they had known him intimately. I, myself, have met many such persons in the Hebrides.

The following is but a selection from the lesser known folk tales of that period.

Hidden treasure

**There is a tradition that in the *Feadan Mór*, or Great Chanter, a gully
situated on the west of Sutherland, there lies concealed a hogshead of
gold said to have been sent from France to finance the arduous undertaking of the Jacobites during 'the Forty-five.'**

The hogshead was consigned to a certain Duncan MacRae. Duncan
was endowed with the second-sight; and forby he had the faculty of rendering invisible both persons and objects when he did not wish them to be seen.
So as to ensure the safe custody of the hogshead of gold, Duncan and a couple of his confederates conveyed it to the fastnesses of the *Feadan Mór*.
There they buried it, hoping that, if one day Prince Charlie should happen to
find himself in this part of Sutherland, it might be of service to him.

But Prince Charlie never came this way. And, so, to this day, they
say in the north of Scotland, the hogshead of gold lies buried in the *Feadan
Mór*.

Now, Duncan put a spell on the hogshead - a spell that made it invisible to the human eye except for a brief moment once in seven years.

Somewhere about 1845 - just a century after Duncan had concealed
this treasure - a crofter woman sat watching her cows, as they grazed in the
vicinity of the *Feadan Mór*. As she sat, she spun; and, as she spun, she suddenly noticed by her side part of a hogshead projecting from the ground.
Believing that at long last the buried treasure of 'the Forty-five' had become
visible once more, she drove her distaff into the ground beside the hogshead,
in order the more readily to identify the position, and then hastened to her
native village to inform the neighbours of her discovery.

In great excitement the villagers now followed her to the *Feadan
Mór*. But on returning there with them, she could locate neither the
hogshead nor her distaff. Both had vanished, for, though Duncan Macrae
had been dead long since, his power of rendering things invisible still per-
vaded the *Feadan Mór*, and maintained the hogshead under spell.

And, so, to this day the treasure sent from France to assist the cause
of a hapless Prince lies among the wilds of Sutherland.

Treasure in Coire Scamadale

At Scamadale, on Loch Hourn, is the site of the home in which, it is said, lived one of the Seven Strong Men of Scotland at the time of 'the Fifteen.' This particular warrior, when on the point of leaving his home for Sheriffmuir, buried all his treasure in a corrie above Scamadale known as Coire Scamadale. The precise position of the treasure could be located only by the light of the moon when visible from a certain spot. This warrior's name was Rory Mor. At Sheriffmuir he was a casualty; and so his treasure still lies hidden in Coire Scamadale.

A native of the district, who now resides by the shores of Loch Nevis, the fiord to the south of Loch Hourn, is known to have spent many moonlight nights in search of this treasure. It is told of this man that, when chasing a hind in the corrie one day, his foot touched a spot at which it seemed as though the treasure lay, judging by the jingling sound he heard. But he was too intent at the time in pursuing his quarry, and thought now that in any case he could identify the spot with ease.

The hind got away from him; and, when he endeavoured to return to the spot where he thought his foot had disturbed the treasure of Rory Mor, he could not find it. Never before was man more regretful that he had not let the hind go her own way earlier in the chase.

The Appin dirk

In Argyll there is a queer story told of the Appin dirk and its association with Culloden. Somewhere about the month of June, in the fateful year 1746, a band of Redcoats, while on its way to Inveraray through Appin, pillaged and plundered as it went. In moving through the Strath of Appin one evening, one of the band noticed a young woman milking her cows in a field by the roadside. Without either explanation or provocation, the sergeant in charge leapt over the dyke, and shot a cow dead. He then directed his attention to the young woman, who defended herself with great wit and courage.

As she was forced to retreat toward the Appin shore, she picked up a stone. This she hurled at the sergeant with such force and accuracy that it stunned him, thus allowing her to escape to a boat afloat by the water-line.

She rowed out to an island for safety; and there she remained until she felt herself free to return, and not likely to incur any further danger at the hands of the Redcoats. This heroine's name is given in Appin as Julia MacColl.

The stunned sergeant was soon picked up by his men, and conveyed to a place of halt for the night. By morning he had succumbed to the wound inflicted by the stone thrown by Julia MacColl. His corpse was interred in the old churchyard at Airds. But the men of Appin decided that his body should not remain there a moment longer than could be helped. So, when the Redcoats had gone their way, they exhumed the body of the sergeant, and flung it into the sea - but not before Julia MacColl's brother had flayed the right arm of it with a view to making from the skin a dirk-sheath.

When this self-same dirk-sheath was seen by the Rev. Alexander Stewart (known throughout the Highlands and Islands as 'Nether Lochaber,' his pseudonym), it was dark brown in colour, limp and soft to the touch, and bore no ornamentation except a small piece of brass at the point, and a thin edging of brass round the opening, on which were inscribed the date, 1747, and the initials D.C.M.

It is nearly seventy years since Dr. Stewart handled this grim relic of 'the Forty-five.' There is no trace of it in Appin today. But some years ago a number of MacColls emigrated from these parts to New Zealand; and among them were two or three Julias. And so it is thought that the dirk and sheath may now be in the keeping of Julia MacColl's descendants at the other side of the earth. If this be the case, they form an interesting, though gruesome, link with Appin and 'the Forty-five.'

A pedlar's fate

Several well-known traditions and folk tales associated with Prince Charlie are still recounted by the older inhabitants of Glen Moriston. The story is told of a pedlar who, in passing through the glen, was shot dead by a band of soldiers who took him to be the Prince - so strongly did he resemble the latter in facial expression. (No explanation is forthcoming as to why they took the pedlar's life when they could have taken him alive with the greatest ease, if they seriously thought him to be Prince Charlie).

The officer in charge immediately had the pedlar's head cut off. With this head he proceeded triumphantly to the Duke of Cumberland, who at the time was at Fort Augustus. Perhaps he expected to receive the substantial reward offered for Charlie, dead or alive!

The story continues that Cumberland exhibited the head to a number of Jacobite prisoners then incarcerated at Fort Augustus, and enquired of them whether they recognised it to be the head of their Prince. 'It is, indeed,' they murmured, hoping that in so doing they might be giving to the fugitive some brief respite from pursuit.

The spot in Glen Moriston, at which the innocent pedlar met his death, is marked by a cairn.

Charlie's outlaws

After the rout of the clans at Culloden, a small band of Glen Moriston men, whose homes had been razed because of their allegiance to the Stuarts, took upon themselves the vow that never would they conclude their peace with the House of Hanover. And they took up their abode in a cave on the hillside, a goodly way up the glen. Here they lived the lives of outlaws, spending as much of their time as possible in harrying the Redcoats and their dependants. For a while Prince Charlie rested with these men during one of his flights; and it was while the Prince sojourned with them in this cave that he had occasion to reprimand them for their swearing and cursing.

Nearly two hundred years have passed by since Charlie came this way; but even to this day tales are told of the Seven Men of Glen Moriston. Their number consisted of three Chisholms, two MacDonalds, one MacGregor, and one Grant. These men had banded themselves together into 'a small association of offence and defence against the Duke of Cumberland and his army (he and the Laird of Grant having betrayed so many of their countrymen upon giving up their arms) never to yield but to die on the spot, never to give up their arms, and that for all the days of their lives.'

The Seven Men of Glen Moriston confined their attention not merely to harassing or killing any Redcoats that came their way, but also to inflicting summary vengeance upon any Highlander whom they believed to have been guilty of conspiring with the enemy. And it was to the custody of these dauntless fellows that MacDonald of Glenaladale committed Prince Charlie at a later stage in his wanderings. One of the Seven Men soon recognised their charge. His name was John MacDonald.

'At the sight of him the poor man changed colours,' says Iain Og of Borrodale of John MacDonald, 'and turned as red as blood, and addressed him in the following manner: 'I am sorry to see you in such a poor state, and hope if I live to see you yet in a better condition, as I have seen you before at the head of your army, upon the green of Glasgow: all I can do is to continue faithful to you while I live, and I am willing to leave my wife and children and follow you wherever you incline going.' '

A family wiped out

Let me draw this volume to a close with a brief folk tale associated with the sandy foreshore at Barrisdale, on Loch Hourn, that used to be renowned for its oyster-beds.

At the time of the Rising, one of the MacKenzies of Seaforth, who is said to have exercised suzerainty over this part of Knoydart, frequently toured his domain in search of young men of military age, and capable of bearing arms. There lived at Barrisdale at this time an aged widow, from whom he already had taken seven sons to fight in his wars and feuds. All these sons were killed eventually.

When next Seaforth visited this district, the widow reproached him for his having robbed her of everything she had in life, but challenged him to deprive her of that stretch of the foreshore so rich in oysters and other shellfish, from which she derived much of her diet. Local lore has it that, in retaliation for this rebuke, Seaforth directed a number of his men to proceed to the foreshore with ploughs, to turn up and destroy the oyster-beds; but it is said that, despite Seaforth's vindictiveness, the widow survived at Barrisdale for many a day.

She used to mention that the three most dreadful experiences of her life were the cold fog of November, the frost that comes in May, and the sight of the vindictive Seaforth.

During the feuds that obsessed the Highlanders in olden times, it was no unusual occurrence for one clan to seek revenge on a neighbouring clan by ploughing up or otherwise destroying beaches noted for their abundance of shellfish. There is a tradition in the Parish of the Small Isles that a band of men, hostile to the MacDonalds of Clan Ranald, thus devastated the shellfish beach fringing the Singing Sands of Laig Bay, in the Isle of Eigg.

Scottish bestsellers from Lang Syne

Scottish Proverbs
ISBN 978-0-94626-408-7
£5.99

Nessie's Monster Activity Book
ISBN 978-1-85217-088-2
£3.99

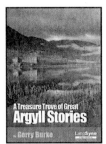

Prophecies of the Brahan Seer
ISBN 978-1-85217-136-0
£5.99

A Treasure Trove of Great Argyll Stories
ISBN 978-1-85217-176-6
£5.99

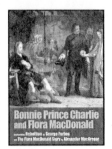

Flight of the Midgie
ISBN 978-1-85217-116-2
£4.99

Bonnie Prince Charlie and Flora MacDonald
ISBN 978-1-85217-008-0
£5.99

Nessie – My story
ISBN 978-0-94626-415-5
£2.50

Strange old Scots customs and superstitions
ISBN 978-0-946264-056
£5.99